ALL I WANT FOR CHRISTMAS

A SHORT HOLIDAY ROMANCE

COME HOME FOR CHRISTMAS
BOOK FOUR

SYLVIA MCDANIEL

Coming Home for Christmas

I'll Be Home for Christmas
White Christmas
Santa's Baby
All I Want For Christmas
Box Set

Love books? Love deals? Love a little mischief? Sign up for my Substack—it's free!

https://sylviamcdanielauthor.substack.com/

In the Honeymoon Suite of Life, Love has Other Plans

Dr. Noah Baker and Dr. Hannah Young share a deep, unshakable friendship bound by their love for medicine. But the unspoken attraction between them remains a line they're hesitant to cross.

Noah carries the scars of his adoptive parents' professional rivalry that destroyed their personal lives. He's determined not to repeat their mistakes, especially with Hannah, who's become an essential part of his world.

Their lives take an unexpected turn when Noah goes to visit his father for Christmas and proposes that Hannah pretends to be his partner to protect their friendship. But Hannah craves more than a mere charade.

As they land in Missoula, an unforeseen blizzard traps them in a hotel's honeymoon suite, forcing them into four days of close quarters. Insta-love sparks, the line between a fake and real relationship blurs, challenging Noah and Hannah to confront their deepest desires and fears.

The storm raging outside is nothing compared to the emotions igniting within.Can their friendship survive when a fake relationship turns real?

CHAPTER 1

$\mathcal{N}$oah Baker stood at the rental car counter in Missoula Regional Airport, his jaw clenched so tight it ached, and tried very hard not to lose his temper with the woman behind the computer screen.

He refused to let her ruin this trip. He absolutely refused.

For the first time in five years, five long, complicated years, he was going to spend Christmas with his father. His father and the new wife Noah had never met. After everything they'd been through with his mother, after all the chaos and dysfunction and barely controlled madness that had defined his childhood, his father finally seemed happy.

Noah wanted to be there. Needed to be there. Needed to see with his own eyes that his father had found some measure of peace.

"I specifically rented a four-wheel drive vehicle in case of bad weather," Noah said, keeping his voice level through sheer force of will. "I understand Montana winters. That's why I made arrangements ahead of time."

The rental agent, Stacy, according to her name tag, looked at him with the patient expression of someone who'd had this conversation twenty times already today. "Sir, I understand your frustration. Your vehicle is ready and waiting. But what I'm trying to tell you is that you cannot leave Missoula. The highway between here and Whitefish is closed. Not just inadvisable, closed. As in gates down and locked."

She slid a piece of paper across the counter with a hotel name and phone number written on it. "I strongly suggest you call this hotel right now and book a room before they sell out completely."

Noah stared at her, trying to process the words. Closed? How could they close an entire highway before a storm even started? And hotel rooms selling out, that happened for concerts or conventions, not snowstorms.

"What do you mean, sell out?" Even to his own ears, his voice sounded incredulous.

Stacy's expression shifted from patient to concerned. "Sir, the biggest storm of the decade is expected to hit in the next few hours. Right now, there are still a few hotel rooms available in Missoula. In about an hour, this city is going to be flooded with stranded travelers, and there won't be anything left." She paused. "You can take your vehicle if you want, but you won't get out of town. The highway patrol isn't letting anyone through."

She was talking to him, a doctor, someone with an M.D. after his name, someone who'd survived medical school and residency, like he was an idiot who couldn't understand basic cause and effect.

And maybe he was being an idiot. Maybe growing up in Houston, where winter meant putting on a light jacket, had left him completely unprepared for the reality of Montana in December.

This was supposed to be his first Christmas with his father since the old man had remarried. The first Christmas that felt like it might actually be pleasant instead of a minefield of his mother's unpredictable moods. He'd been looking forward to it for months.

"Noah."

He turned to find Hannah already on her phone, stepping away from the counter to make a call. Of course, she was. While he stood there arguing with reality, his best friend was already solving the problem.

This was why they worked so well together. Noah got caught up in the details, in what should be happening versus what was actually happening. Hannah just rolled with whatever came at them and found solutions.

He watched her talk on the phone, watched her blonde hair catch the fluorescent lights, watched the way she gestured with one hand while holding her phone with the other, watched her laugh at something the person on the other end said.

Six years. They'd been friends for six years. Partners. Study buddies in medical school, support systems during residency, and now colleagues at one of Houston's busiest emergency rooms. And in all that time, he'd never crossed the line from friendship to something more.

Even though he'd wanted to. God, how he'd wanted to.

"Yes, ma'am," Hannah was saying into her phone. "We just landed at the airport, and the rental agency is telling us we need to find a hotel room immediately. Do you have anything available?"

She paused, listening, and then she started laughing, that bright, genuine laugh that always made something in Noah's chest feel lighter.

"All right, we'll take it. Let me give you a credit card number to hold the reservation." She rattled off numbers from memory. "Perfect. We'll be there as soon as we leave the airport. Thank you so much."

She ended the call and turned back to him, triumphant. "Done. Got us a room."

"Thank you," Noah said to Stacy, who looked relieved that at least one of them was being reasonable.

Hannah grabbed his arm and steered him away from the counter. Behind them, Noah could see a long line of increasingly anxious travelers waiting to rent vehicles, all of them probably about to get the same news he'd just received.

Maybe he should be grateful they had a Jeep and, apparently, a hotel room. Maybe fighting reality wasn't the best use of his energy.

"When we get the vehicle, I want you to check the local news websites," Noah said as they walked toward the exit. "Verify that the roads are actually closed. I still can't believe they'd shut down a major highway before the storm even hits."

Hannah stopped walking and turned to face him, one eyebrow raised in that expression he knew meant she thought he was being ridiculous. "Noah. You've never lived anywhere that gets real snowstorms. In Wyoming, where I grew up, remember? —they have actual gates that lock across the roads. Not suggestions. Not warnings. Physical barriers. Because people like you, intelligent, educated, stubborn people, would absolutely try to drive through blizzards and then need to be rescued."

"I wouldn't—"

"You would," she said flatly. "You're doing it right now. You're literally planning to double-check the news reports because you don't believe what multiple people have told you."

Noah opened his mouth to argue, then closed it again. She was right. Of course she was right.

"I just wanted to get to Whitefish," he said quietly. "I wanted to see my dad. Meet his new wife. It's been so long since we've spent real time together. Since before Mom—" He couldn't finish that sentence either.

Hannah's expression softened. She reached out and squeezed his arm. "I know. And we will get there. Just maybe not today."

They found their rental Jeep in the lot and loaded their suitcases. The sky above them was grey and heavy, the kind of grey that promised snow and lots of it. The temperature had dropped significantly since they'd landed thirty minutes ago.

Noah was grateful Hannah had agreed to come with him on this trip. She didn't have family to visit for Christmas, her parents had retired to Arizona and were on a cruise, and when he'd mentioned his plans, she'd offered to tag along for moral support.

"Meeting the new stepmother seems like it might be stressful," she'd said. "You might need backup."

She'd been joking, but she wasn't wrong. His father's happiness was wonderful, but it also meant Noah had to navigate a new family dynamic, had to figure out where he fit in this new configuration. Having Hannah there would make it easier. She made everything easier.

As they climbed into the Jeep, Hannah already had her phone out, pulling up the Montana Department of Transportation website. "Yep. All highways between Missoula and White-fish: closed due to severe weather and blowing snow. The storm is already hitting the northern part of the state." She looked up at him. "We're officially stuck. But hey, at least I got us a room."

"How many rooms?" Noah asked, starting the engine.

"One." Hannah didn't look up from her phone. "That was all they had left. I had to give them a credit card number immedi-ately to hold it, or it would've been gone before we got there."

One room.

They'd been friends for six years and had never shared a room. Never even come close. There had been an unspoken boundary between them, a line neither of them had crossed because crossing it would change everything.

And Noah had spent six years very carefully not changing anything.

He'd watched his parents destroy each other. Both doctors. Both brilliant. Both so consumed by their work and their egos and their need to be right that they'd created a home that felt more like a war zone than a family.

His mother especially. She'd been what the psychiatrists had eventually called "psychotic with narcissistic features." However, that clinical diagnosis didn't begin to capture what it was like to grow up in the crossfire of her mood swings and delusions.

Noah had learned early that relationships between doctors were dangerous. That working together and sleeping together created a toxic mixture of competition and resentment. That loving someone you also had to professionally respect was a recipe for disaster.

So he'd kept things with Hannah firmly in the friend zone. Even when he wanted more. Even when he caught himself staring at her across the ER, admiring the way she handled patients, the way she made split-second decisions that saved lives. Even when he went out with other women and found himself comparing them all to Hannah and finding them lacking.

He drove through the small mountain town, following the GPS directions to the hotel Hannah had booked. The snowflakes were starting to fall now, just a few at first, then more, then suddenly so many that it was like someone had torn open a pillow and dumped the contents from the sky.

"I think snow-mageddon has arrived," Noah said, watching the flakes swirl in his headlights.

"And you wanted to drive to Whitefish in this," Hannah said, shaking her head. "Yeah, that would've gone well."

"Point taken."

They pulled up under the hotel awning just as the storm kicked into high gear. Through the windshield, Noah could barely see the building in front of them.

"Let me get the suitcases," Hannah said, already climbing out. "You park the car."

But when they walked into the lobby, the frazzled clerk

behind the desk looked at them with an expression somewhere between relief and panic.

"You must be Dr. Reeves," she said to Hannah. "Thank God you're here. The manager wanted to give your room away to someone else, and I told him it was already reserved. But we're completely full now. The only room we have available is the honeymoon suite. Is that... is that okay?"

Noah felt his stomach drop. The honeymoon suite. Of course it was.

"You don't have anything else?" he asked, hearing the edge in his voice. "Two rooms? Two beds?"

"Sir, you're lucky to still have this room," the clerk said. "We've been sold out for the past hour. People are sleeping in the lobby."

Hannah laughed, that same easy laugh that meant she found the whole situation amusing instead of catastrophic. "We'll take it. And all the perks that come with it."

The clerk smiled with visible relief and quickly made key cards. "Wonderful. Tonight we'll bring up chocolate-covered strawberries and champagne. It's all included in the honeymoon package."

Perfect. Exactly what they didn't need.

They took the elevator to the third floor, neither of them speaking. Noah could feel tension radiating off his own body, could feel his carefully maintained boundaries starting to crack.

He opened the door to the suite and stopped dead.

It was exactly what he'd feared. A king-sized bed with rose petals scattered across the comforter. Dim lighting designed for romance. A heart-shaped jacuzzi tub visible through an open bathroom door. Mirrors on the ceiling. Champagne already chilling in an ice bucket.

A love playground.

"What the hell," Noah breathed. "We can't stay here."

Hannah walked past him into the room, setting down her suitcase and looking around with undisguised amusement. She touched the rose petals on the bed, then walked over to examine the jacuzzi.

"Why not?" she said, turning to grin at him. "I think this looks like fun. Besides, what choice do we have? Sleep in the lobby?"

Noah stared at her, trying to read her expression. Was she serious? Was this actually not bothering her at all?

"Go move the car from under the awning," Hannah said, already unzipping her suitcase. "I'll unpack while you're gone. Get us settled."

He fled.

It took him ten minutes to find a parking spot in the increasingly packed lot, and by the time he jogged back to the hotel, the storm had turned into a complete whiteout. He could barely see five feet in front of him. Snow was already piling up in drifts against the building.

They weren't going anywhere. Not tonight. Probably not tomorrow either.

Noah stood in the hallway outside the honeymoon suite for a long moment, trying to calm his racing heart, trying to convince himself that this was fine. They were adults. They were professionals. They could share a room for one night without it meaning anything.

He unlocked the door and stepped inside.

And froze.

Hannah was in the jacuzzi. Naked, or at least, he had to assume she was naked beneath the thick layer of bubbles that covered her from neck to toes. Her blonde hair was piled on top of her head, a few strands escaping to curl against her neck. Her head was tilted back against the edge of the tub, her eyes closed, her skin flushed from the heat.

She looked like every fantasy he'd spent six years trying not to have.

"Oh good, you're back," Hannah said, opening her eyes and smiling at him. "Come on in. The water is perfect. And look—"

She gestured to the side of the tub where two champagne flutes sat next to a plate of chocolate-covered strawberries. "They already delivered the perks."

Noah swallowed hard. His mouth had gone completely dry. "Hannah—"

"Noah." She sat up slightly, and he quickly averted his eyes, afraid of what he might see. "We're stuck here. In a snowstorm. In a honeymoon suite. We might as well enjoy it, right?"

"We're friends," he said, the words coming out hoarse. "Colleagues."

"I know." Her voice was soft now, serious. "But maybe we could be more than that. If you wanted to be."

His heart was pounding so hard he could hear it in his ears. "If I get in that tub with you—"

"Then everything changes," Hannah finished. "I know. But Noah, maybe it's time for things to change. Maybe we've been holding back for long enough."

He stared at her, at the invitation in her eyes, at six years of carefully maintained boundaries hovering on the edge of collapse.

And for the first time in his adult life, Noah stopped overthinking and just felt.

"Okay," he said.

<h1 style="text-align:center">CHAPTER 2</h1>

Hannah Young had loved Noah Baker for four years, and she was done waiting.

She'd tried patience. She'd tried subtlety. She'd tried being the perfect friend, the ideal colleague, the woman who understood him better than anyone else in the world. And what had it gotten her? More of the same careful distance, more of those moments when his eyes would linger on her face just a second too long before he'd look away, more of that almost-unbearable tension that neither of them ever acknowledged.

Well, tonight that changed. One way or another.

She watched him standing in the doorway of the honeymoon suite, staring at her in the jacuzzi like a man who'd just realized he'd walked into the wrong room. Except it wasn't the wrong room. It was exactly the right room, with exactly the right setup, and if he couldn't see that, then she'd been wasting four years of her life.

The thought made something twist painfully in her chest.

"What are you doing?" His voice came out rough, uncertain in a way that Noah's voice almost never was.

Hannah forced herself to smile, to keep her tone light and

casual even though her heart was hammering against her ribs. "Soaking in the tub. There's room for two, if you're interested."

She could see him processing this, could practically watch the gears turning in that brilliant, analytical mind of his. He was probably already running through a dozen scenarios, weighing outcomes, calculating risks. That was Noah's problem, he thought too much. He let his fear of becoming his parents override everything else, even his own happiness.

Even *them*.

"Hannah, we can't—" he started.

"Can't what?" She sat up slightly, making sure to keep the bubbles positioned strategically. She wasn't trying to seduce him with nudity, not yet, anyway. She was trying to show him that taking this step didn't have to be terrifying. That they could handle this like they handled everything else: together. "Can't you enjoy a perfectly good jacuzzi tub? Can't drink the champagne that came with the room? Can't spend one evening relaxing instead of overthinking everything?"

He ran a hand through his dark hair, making it stand up in the way it always did when he was stressed. "You know what I mean."

"Actually, I don't." That was a lie. She knew exactly what he meant. But she was tired of pretending that the elephant in the room didn't exist. Tired of dancing around the truth that had been obvious to everyone except, apparently, Noah himself. "Why don't you spell it out for me?"

Noah opened his mouth, then closed it again. He looked away from her, his jaw working like he was grinding his teeth. Through the window behind him, snow was falling so heavily that the parking lot below had disappeared into white static.

They were trapped here. Together. And Hannah had never been more grateful for a Montana blizzard in her life.

"Are you cold?" she asked, gentling her voice. This wasn't supposed to feel like an interrogation. "You look like you're freezing."

"It's really coming down out there," he said, still not meeting her eyes. "If it starts lightning, you should get out of the water."

Hannah nearly laughed. Leave it to Noah to worry about winter thunderstorms while she was sitting here naked, offering him everything he claimed he didn't want. "The hot water will warm you up," she said. "I poured you a glass of champagne."

She watched him hesitate, watched the war playing out across his face. Part of him wanted to run, she could see it in the way he was angled toward the door, in the tension in his shoulders. But part of him wanted to stay. Wanted *her*. She'd seen that look in his eyes before, in unguarded moments when he thought she wasn't paying attention.

He turned his back to her and started removing his coat.

Hannah let out a breath she hadn't realized she was holding. Step one: accomplished. Now came the hard part.

She studied him while he undressed, noting the familiar lines of his shoulders, the way his hands moved with the careful precision he brought to everything. In the ER, those hands saved lives. She'd watched him suture wounds that would have taken other doctors twice as long, watched him perform procedures with a confidence that came from thousands of hours of practice.

But right now, those same hands were shaking slightly as he unlaced his boots.

"Hannah, are you certain we should do this?"

The uncertainty in his voice made her want to climb out of this ridiculous heart-shaped tub and shake him. Of course, she was certain. She'd been certain for years. She was so certain that she'd packed condoms in her suitcase before leaving Houston, just in case. She was so certain that when the hotel clerk had mentioned the honeymoon suite, she'd felt a surge of triumph instead of awkwardness.

This weekend was make-or-break time. Either Noah finally opened his eyes and saw what was right in front of him, or Hannah was done waiting. She'd already looked into positions at other hospitals, Oklahoma City, where her extended family lived. Tulsa. Even Denver. Places far enough from Houston that she wouldn't have to watch Noah date other women, wouldn't have to pretend it didn't hurt every time he came back from a failed dinner date and complained that the woman "just didn't get it."

She got it. She'd always gotten it. He was just too scared to let her prove it.

"Get in the tub, Noah," she said, keeping her voice firm. "We're going to soak, drink champagne, and relax. That's all."

That was not all, but he didn't need to know that yet.

He sat on the bed to remove his boots and socks, moving with exaggerated care. Hannah suppressed a smile. She'd seen Noah naked before, it was impossible to avoid in the chaos of the hospital locker room, where privacy was a luxury no one could afford. She'd caught glimpses of his body during hurried scrub changes: the muscles in his back, his flat stomach, the thin trail of dark hair that disappeared below his waistband.

Once, she'd even seen his cock, just for a second before she'd jerked her gaze away, her face burning.

She wasn't looking away tonight.

Noah stood and unbuttoned his jeans, then glanced back at her. "Close your eyes."

Hannah wanted to laugh. They were both doctors. They'd both seen more naked bodies than most people saw in a lifetime. But fine. If it made him feel better, she'd play along.

She closed her eyes and heard the rustle of fabric, the soft splash as he stepped into the tub. The water level rose as he settled into the opposite side of the heart shape, and when Hannah opened her eyes again, he was staring up at the mirrored ceiling with an expression somewhere between amusement and horror.

"This has got to be a safety hazard," he said. "Can you imagine trying to get out of this thing in the dark? Someone's going to slip and crack their head open. I wonder how many ER visits this hotel is responsible for annually."

There he was, Dr. Noah Baker, always thinking three steps ahead, always cataloging potential disasters. Hannah took a sip of her champagne and let the bubbles fizz on her tongue. She didn't usually drink much; alcohol and medicine were a dangerous combination, and she'd seen too many brilliant careers derailed by addiction. But tonight, she needed the liquid courage.

Tonight, she needed to be brave enough for both of them.

"We'll leave a light on," she said. "Problem solved."

The bathroom fell quiet except for the low hum of the jacuzzi jets and the distant howl of wind outside. They were on the top floor, insulated from whatever chaos was unfolding in the hotel below. Hannah had glimpsed the lobby on their way up, it had been packed with stranded travelers, families with crying children, elderly couples looking exhausted and worried.

She and Noah were lucky. They had this room, this moment, this chance.

All she had to do was make him see it.

"You know, this is actually nice," Noah said after a moment. His voice had relaxed slightly, some of the tension bleeding out of it. "The hot water feels good after being out in that cold."

"The champagne isn't bad either," Hannah agreed. "Remember graduation night? We split a bottle of champagne and you kept insisting we should do it 'properly' with the fancy flutes and the toasts."

"I remember Match Day better," Noah said, and there was a smile in his voice now. "When we found out we'd both matched to the same hospital for residency. That was, God, that was such a relief. I don't think I could have gotten through those years without you."

The words hung in the air between them, weighted with meaning that Noah probably didn't even realize he was giving them. That was the thing about him, he could be so emotionally intelligent with patients, so perceptive about what they needed, but completely blind to his own feelings.

Or maybe not blind. Maybe just determined to ignore them.

Hannah picked up her champagne glass and held it up. "Let's do a toast."

Noah raised his glass to meet hers. In the dim lighting of the bathroom, with steam rising around them and snow falling outside, it felt almost dreamlike. Unreal. Like they'd stepped outside their normal lives into some alternate version of reality where taking risks was allowed.

"To having the best Christmas ever with your father and stepmother," Hannah said. Then, before she could lose her nerve: "And to love."

They clinked glasses. Noah took a sip, then lowered his glass with a slight frown. "Why love?"

Here it was. The opening she'd been waiting for. Hannah took a breath and dove in.

"Because we both need it. We're almost thirty, Noah. We're successful doctors with good careers and nice apartments and everything we're supposed to want. But we're missing something. At least, I am." She paused, watching his face. "I've been thinking about the future lately. If I want kids, I need to start making decisions soon. And that means finding someone to build a life with."

Noah nodded slowly. "It's not easy, though. I've tried dating. Hell, I've tried really hard. But no one—" He stopped, seeming to reconsider his words. "They're either not intellectually compatible, or we just don't connect. I tried explaining a case to someone last month, this guy came in with internal bleeding, and we had to do emergency surgery right there in the ER, and she just stared at me with this glazed look. Like I was speaking a foreign language."

Hannah couldn't help it; she laughed. "That's because you *were* speaking a foreign language to her. Most people don't want to hear about emergency surgeries over dinner."

"But it's what I do," Noah protested. "It's a huge part of my life. How am I supposed to be with someone who doesn't understand that?"

"You're not," Hannah said quietly. "That's the point. You need someone who gets it. Someone who's lived it. Someone who speaks the same language you do."

She let the words settle, let him work through the logic. This was how Noah processed information, methodically, carefully, building his understanding piece by piece until suddenly the whole picture became clear.

"That's why we work so well as friends," he said after a moment. "We have medicine in common. We can talk about our cases, compare notes. You understand the pressure, the responsibility. You know what it's like to hold someone's life in your hands and know that one wrong decision could end it."

"I do know," Hannah said. "And that's exactly my point."

She watched comprehension flicker across his face, then watched him push it away. Not yet. He wasn't ready yet.

"If you get married," Noah said slowly, "would your husband understand our connection? Our friendship?"

Hannah nearly threw her champagne glass at him.

Was he serious? Was he actually sitting here, naked in a heart-shaped jacuzzi tub with her, asking about her hypothetical *husband*? Was he really that oblivious?

Or was he testing her? Trying to figure out if she felt the same way he did?

"That's an interesting question," she said, keeping her voice level through sheer force of will. "Let me ask you the same thing. What if I called you at three in the morning to consult on a case? Would your wife think we were having an affair?"

Noah went very still. His eyes locked on hers, and for the first time all evening, she saw real understanding there. Real awareness of what was happening between them.

Good. It was about damn time.

Hannah reached for the plate of chocolate-covered strawberries the hotel had provided and selected one. She bit into it slowly, savoring the sweetness, the way the chocolate melted on her tongue. When she looked up, Noah was watching her with an intensity that made heat bloom in her stomach that had nothing to do with the hot water.

"Close your eyes," she said softly.

"Why?"

"Because I'm asking you to. Trust me."

After a long moment, Noah closed his eyes. Hannah picked up another strawberry and leaned forward, closing the distance between them. She traced the chocolate-covered fruit across his lips, watching his mouth part slightly, watching his throat work as he swallowed.

"That tastes good," he murmured.

Then Hannah kissed him.

His lips were soft and tasted like chocolate and champagne. She licked the strawberry juice from his chin, felt him inhale sharply, felt the exact moment when his control finally, *finally* broke.

"Hannah," he gasped, pulling back just enough to speak. "We're friends."

She was done being friends. She was done waiting. She was done pretending that this wasn't what they both wanted.

Hannah moved through the water until she was straddling him, until her wet skin was pressed against his, until there was no mistaking the hard length of his erection against her thigh.

"It's time we were more than friends," she said, looking directly into his eyes. "It's time for you to stop being scared. It's time for you to let yourself have what you want."

For one terrible second, she thought he might push her away. Thought he might retreat into that safe distance he always maintained.

Then his arms came up around her, pulling her against him with a groan that sounded like surrender and triumph all at once.

"God, Hannah," he breathed against her mouth. "Do you have any idea how long—"

She kissed him again, harder this time, pouring four years of frustration and longing into it. "I know," she whispered. "I know exactly how long. And we're not waiting anymore."

His hands slid up her back, into her wet hair, and when he kissed her back, it was with all the passion he'd been holding back for years.

Finally. *Finally.*

Outside, the storm raged on. But inside this ridiculous honeymoon suite, with its heart-shaped tub and mirrored ceiling and scattered rose petals, Hannah Young was exactly where she wanted to be.

And she wasn't letting go.

CHAPTER 3

For years, Noah had avoided his feelings for Hannah because he'd watched his parents destroy each other.

Two brilliant doctors. Two strong personalities. One medical practice that became a battlefield.

He could still remember lying in bed at night, pillow over his head, trying to block out the sound of them screaming at each other downstairs. Arguments about treatment protocols that devolved into personal attacks. Disagreements about patient care that turned into accusations of incompetence. Professional competition that poisoned everything it touched, until there was nothing left but resentment and rage.

His mother had dissolved the practice when he was in high school. Just walked away from his father, from their shared work, from everything they'd built together. That part, Noah could understand, sometimes things didn't work out, sometimes people needed to go their separate ways.

But she'd also walked away from Noah.

That was the part he couldn't forgive. Couldn't understand, even now, fifteen years later. It was one thing to end a marriage, to close a practice. It was another thing entirely to abandon your seventeen-year-old son because staying in the same city as your ex-husband was too uncomfortable.

She'd moved to Seattle. Sent birthday cards. Called on holidays, when she remembered. Built a new life that had no room in it for the child she'd left behind.

Thank God he'd been old enough to cope. Old enough to finish high school, apply to colleges, plan for medical school. Old enough to know that her leaving said everything about her and nothing about him.

But not old enough to escape the lesson she'd taught him: that doctors who worked together inevitably destroyed each other. That loving someone you also had to professionally respect was a recipe for disaster.

So he'd made himself a rule: never get involved with another doctor. Keep those worlds separate. Don't risk turning into his parents.

And yet.

Hannah was his best friend. Had been for years. She was brilliant, compassionate, funny, grounded, everything he'd ever wanted in a partner. She was also the only woman he'd been attracted to in any meaningful way, which made dating other people an exercise in futility. Every woman he met was compared to Hannah and found wanting.

It wasn't fair to them. It wasn't fair to himself. And it definitely wasn't fair to Hannah, who deserved better than being the impossible standard no one else could meet.

Did he dare take the risk? Did he dare break his own rule for her?

What if it ended badly? What if they became his parents, tearing each other apart over professional disagreements? What if he lost not just a lover, but his best friend?

But then Hannah was in his arms, her body pressed against his, and all those careful calculations evaporated like steam. His lips found hers and suddenly none of his rules mattered. None of his fears mattered. The only thing that mattered was this: the taste of her mouth, the feel of her skin, the way she fit against him like she'd been designed specifically for this purpose.

This was exactly what he'd been afraid of. This total loss of control. This complete inability to think rationally when she was near him.

And God help him, he didn't want to stop.

He couldn't let this end. Couldn't pull back, couldn't retreat into safety. His body had made the decision his mind had been avoiding for years, and there was no going back now. She could feel his response to her, there was no hiding it, no pretending this was just friendly affection.

They'd crossed the line. Finally, irrevocably, they'd crossed it.

Hannah was the most intelligent, most beautiful woman he'd ever known. They'd been through everything together: the brutal grind of medical school, the soul-crushing exhaustion of residency, the triumph of their first successful emergency procedures. She'd been there for every major moment of his adult life.

When he had a complicated case and needed to talk through the options, Hannah was who he called. When his mother committed suicide, Hannah was the one who'd driven to his apartment at two in the morning and held him while he cried. She'd made him tea, let him talk about his grief, and stayed until sunrise to make sure he wasn't alone.

She'd been his person for so long. Why had he fought so hard against letting her be his person in every way?

Noah cupped her face in his hands and kissed her again, deeper this time, trying to pour four years of denied longing into the contact. He had to taste her, had to memorize every detail of this moment in case his fear caught up with him later and tried to convince him this was a mistake.

Desperation clawed at him. His hands moved over her wet skin, learning the curve of her spine, the dip of her waist, the softness of her everywhere. The urgency thundering through his blood was overwhelming, drowning out every rational thought.

This woman who'd tempted him, tantalized him, soothed him, challenged him, he was done denying what he wanted. Done pretending he could just be her friend. Done letting his parents' dysfunction dictate his future.

Because of them, he'd pushed Hannah away for so long. But with her body against his, with her breath mingling with his, with her hands in his hair pulling him closer, there was no more distance to maintain. No more safety to retreat to.

His mouth claimed hers urgently as he pulled her tighter against him. His hands were everywhere, mapping her body, and the need that exploded through him was almost painful in its intensity. He'd never experienced anything like this. Never felt this combination of desperation and rightness, of hunger and homecoming.

The logical part of his brain noted that a heart-shaped jacuzzi tub was possibly the worst venue for what was about to happen. Terrible ergonomics. High risk of injury. Definitely not recommended by any reasonable medical professional.

But he didn't care.

Four years of suppressed desire was demanding satisfaction, and it was demanding it now. With that first real kiss, every bit of passion he'd kept carefully locked away had broken free, and there was no containing it again.

No more denying he'd wanted her for years. No more making excuses about why they couldn't be together. His body had finally overruled his mind, and honestly, it was a relief.

"Oh God," he breathed against her mouth. "Hannah—"

He knew he wouldn't last long. Not with her hands on him, not with four years of fantasy finally becoming reality. But it didn't matter. Nothing mattered except this moment, the two of them finally pursuing the connection they'd both been avoiding.

No thoughts of tomorrow. No thoughts of consequences. No thoughts of his parents or his rules or what might go wrong.

Just Hannah, and Noah, and the passion he'd tried so hard to contain.

His hand skimmed down the front of her chest, cupping her breast, kneading the soft mound while he ached to wrap his lips around her sweet nipple.

She tasted of erotic dreams and lazy mornings, and everything he tried to withhold from himself. But not today. Not when his need was this crucial. Now when he couldn't wait. Not when she'd started this with them getting naked in this tub.

She pulled his mouth back to her lips, collecting his attention once again while kissing him hungrily.

Right now all he could think about was being inside Hannah. Of pushing deep inside her and taking her to the next plateau. The one where they both reached for the stars. The one where he felt her body wrapped around his cock.

Breaking the kiss, he had to taste her sweet breasts as his lips covered her nipple. A moan escaped her throat as his mouth caressed her breast.

With a quick glance, the fire in her eyes scorched him, and he clenched his fists needing to be inside her now.

"Condoms," he cried.

"Yes," she said as she rose above him.

Gently, he cupped the center of her core while his lips nibbled on her earlobe. His fingers brushed her satiny folds, tempting and teasing while his lips brushed her neck, trailing down her creamy shoulders, sampling her sweet flesh. Her lashes fluttered and he could feel her pulse beneath his lips pounding rhythmically.

And then she gripped his cock in her hand and he feared he would come right then.

"Hannah," he gasped.

Her lips were too tempting as he covered them once again. He didn't want to talk right now. He only wanted to feel, to experience this woman.

The tub was hard, but he lifted her over him, placing his penis at the juncture of her thighs.

"Fuck me," he groaned suddenly not caring that they didn't have a condom. All he wanted was to be inside her.

"Oh, Noah," she whispered into his ear as his fingers delved into her moist depths, preparing her. Needing to be deep inside her. To feel her body lying on his. Feel her flesh around him, pulsing against him.

No thoughts of tomorrow, no thoughts of the next five minutes, only this moment, the two of them pursuing the desire between them. Pursuing the passion he'd tried so hard to contain.

With a primal surge, he entered her, needing to feel her surrounding him, burying himself deep within her.

Her soft whimpers of pleasure increased with each long, slow stroke of his body as he lifted her up and down on his cock.

Hannah had changed him, made him see life from a different angle. His lips covered hers as they shared the breath of life, his nostrils filled with the scent of Hannah, the taste of Hannah on his lips. And he was consumed with a desire that surpassed anything he'd ever felt.

And yet, he knew he was breaking all his rules. They couldn't be in a relationship together and work at the same hospital. It didn't work and he knew from firsthand experience what happened to two strong-minded individuals who worked together.

He clasped her hands in his, bracing against her, plunging deeper and deeper into her, feeling as if his soul was joining with hers. Water from the tub sloshed around them, but he didn't care. This had been such a long time coming, and at this moment, a tornado could roar through the building and he wouldn't stop.

Her eyelashes fluttered against her cheek. Her body quivered as she shuddered with completion.

"Noah," she cried, and his heart swelled. "Now."

God, this woman had a way of making him feel larger than life.

He couldn't hold back any longer. He'd waited as long as he could, but Hannah was ready. Together they reached that pinnacle. Together, they shattered and fell back to the earth. Together, as friends, he had the best sex of his life.

Hannah. Dear God, Hannah.

CHAPTER 4

*H*annah sagged against Noah's chest in the cooling water of the jacuzzi, her body still humming with the aftershocks of what they'd just shared. Her fingers were wrinkled from the water, her muscles felt like warm honey, and her heart was so full she thought it might burst.

This. This was what she'd been waiting for. What she'd dreamed about for four years.

And it had been worth every moment of patience, every failed relationship Noah had with other women, every time she'd bitten her tongue instead of telling him how she felt.

Because this, what they'd just experienced, this was everything.

She tilted her head back to look at him. His eyes were still glazed, his breathing ragged, his hair plastered to his forehead. He looked completely undone, and the sight made something fierce and possessive bloom in her chest.

Mine, she thought. *Finally mine.*

"That was incredible," she said softly.

"Yeah." His voice came out hoarse. "It really was."

Hannah sat up slightly, reality beginning to creep back in

around the edges of her post-orgasmic haze. "We didn't use a condom."

She watched Noah's eyes widen as that fact registered. For a doctor, for someone who spent his professional life preaching safe practices to patients, the lapse was significant.

"I know," he said. "I couldn't—I didn't—"

"I couldn't wait either," Hannah said quickly, not wanting him to spiral into guilt or regret. "It's okay. I'm on birth control, and we're both healthy. We'll be more careful next time."

Next time. She loved the way those words sounded. The assumption that this wasn't a one-off mistake born of champagne and forced proximity. That there would be a next time, and a time after that, and hopefully a lifetime of times.

But she could see Noah's mind starting to work again, could practically watch the gears turning as his rational brain came back online. He'd need time to process what had just happened. Time to work through his fears about becoming his parents, about ruining their friendship, about all the complications of dating a colleague.

Hannah knew him well enough to know that pushing for a conversation now would be a mistake. Noah needed space to think, to analyze, to come to his own conclusions. If she tried to force him to talk about feelings before he was ready, he'd just shut down.

So she'd give him time. She'd let him come to her when he was ready.

"I'm getting out," she said, rising from the water with as much grace as she could manage. Her legs felt shaky. "I'm starving, and I think I saw a mini fridge. Let's see what they have."

She wrapped herself in one of the plush terry cloth robes hanging by the tub and headed into the bathroom, closing the door behind her. The face that looked back at her from the mirror was flushed and glowing, her lips swollen from kissing, her eyes bright.

She looked like a woman who'd just had amazing sex with the man she loved.

Hannah cleaned up efficiently—years of medical training had ingrained certain habits, and preventing UTIs was basic self-care. As she washed her hands, she did a quick mental calculation of where she was in her cycle. Mid-cycle, probably. The timing wasn't ideal for pregnancy, but it wasn't impossible either.

The thought made her pause, one hand pressed to her flat stomach.

A baby. Noah's baby.

The image rose unbidden in her mind: a little boy with Noah's dark hair and serious eyes, or a little girl with his quick mind and careful hands. A child they'd made together, a family they'd build together.

But not like this. Not by accident. Not by trapping him.

If, when, they had children, it would be because they both wanted it. Because Noah had admitted he loved her and couldn't imagine his life without her. Because they'd made a conscious choice together, not because of one moment of passion in a hotel jacuzzi.

Hannah firmly pushed the fantasy aside. One step at a time. First, they needed to figure out what this meant for their relationship. Everything else could wait.

When she emerged from the bathroom, Noah had gotten out of the tub and was wearing the matching robe she'd left for him. He looked more composed now, though his hair was still damp and messy. He was studying the room service menu with the same focused intensity he brought to reading patient charts.

Classic Noah. When emotions got overwhelming, retreat into practical matters.

"Do they have room service?" Hannah asked, keeping her tone light.

"Yeah." He held up the leather-bound menu. "Looks like a full menu, actually. Better than I expected for a hotel in Montana."

Hannah moved to stand beside him, studying the options. Her stomach growled audibly, reminding her that they'd skipped dinner entirely in the chaos of the storm and their impromptu jacuzzi encounter.

"Ooh, they have chicken wings," she said. "And loaded potato skins. I'm hungry, but not 'full meal' hungry. Want to split some appetizers?"

Noah glanced at her, and something in his expression softened. "That sounds perfect."

He called in the order while Hannah pulled back the covers on the enormous bed, noting with amusement that rose petals were still scattered across the pillows. The whole room was so aggressively romantic it was almost funny, like a Valentine's Day card had exploded in here.

But it had served its purpose. They were together now, finally, and whatever came next, they'd figure it out.

"Food should be here in about thirty minutes," Noah said, hanging up the phone. He picked up the remote. "Want to watch something while we wait?"

Hannah climbed onto the bed, arranging the pillows against the headboard. "Sure. Though I'm guessing there's not much on besides weather coverage."

She was right. Noah flipped through channels, and nearly every local station was showing the same thing: storm coverage, emergency warnings, road closures, power outage updates. The meteorologist on screen was practically vibrating with excitement as he pointed to the massive system dumping snow across Montana.

"Heavy snow and blizzard conditions will continue for at least the next forty-eight hours," the meteorologist announced. "We're expecting accumulations of five to six feet in some areas, more than the plows can possibly keep up with. All highways remain closed. Authorities are urging everyone to stay home and off the roads. This is a historic storm, folks. If you're somewhere safe, stay there."

Hannah laughed, shaking her head. "Come to Montana for Christmas, you said. It'll be fun, you said. Meet my dad and his new wife in a charming mountain town."

Noah turned to look at her, and the expression on his face made her breath catch. There was something vulnerable in his eyes, something open and unguarded.

"I'm glad you're here with me," he said quietly.

The words were simple, but the weight behind them was enormous. This was Noah's first real acknowledgment of what had happened between them. His first admission that he didn't regret it, that he wanted her here, that maybe, just maybe, this could be the beginning of something real.

Hannah's heart stuttered in her chest. "Yeah?"

"Yeah." He reached out, and his thumb brushed across her lower lip, wiping away a trace of the lip balm she'd applied in the bathroom. The touch left a trail of heat in its wake. "I don't know what I would have done if I'd been stuck here alone. Probably would have argued with the rental car lady until airport security escorted me out."

"You definitely would have tried to drive to Whitefish and ended up in a ditch," Hannah said, but her voice came out breathless.

"Probably," Noah agreed. His hand cupped her cheek, his thumb stroking along her cheekbone. "But I didn't, because you were here to talk sense into me. Like always."

The moment stretched between them, heavy with unspoken words. Hannah wanted to tell him she loved him. Wanted to ask what this meant for them, where they went from here, whether he could see a future with her the way she'd been seeing one with him for years.

But she held back. Let him set the pace. Let him come to those realizations on his own.

Instead, she leaned into his touch and smiled. "That's what best friends are for."

The word *friends* hung in the air between them, suddenly inadequate for what they were now. But before either of them could address it, there was a knock at the door.

"Room service," a cheerful voice called.

Noah went to answer it, and Hannah watched him interact with the server, noting the way he smiled and thanked them, the way he made sure to tip generously despite the late hour and terrible weather. These were the small kindnesses that made her love him, the way he treated service workers with respect, the way he noticed people even when he was distracted.

He came back with a tray loaded with chicken wings, potato skins, mozzarella sticks, and two bottles of beer. "I figured we could use something more substantial than champagne."

They spread a towel across their laps and dug in, the food warm and satisfying after their eventful evening. The Weather Channel droned on in the background, showing the same storm footage on loop, but Hannah barely noticed. She was too focused on Noah, on the way he kept glancing at her between bites, on the small smile that played at the corners of his mouth.

This felt domestic. Comfortable. Like something they'd done a hundred times before, except now there was an undercurrent of electricity, an awareness of what their bodies had just shared.

"So," Hannah said, dragging a potato skin through sour cream, "your dad's going to wonder where we are."

"I texted him while you were in the bathroom," Noah said. "Told him we were stuck in Missoula until the roads clear. He said not to worry, that we'd have Christmas whenever we got there."

"That's nice of him."

"He's a good guy." Noah's expression softened. "He's been through a lot. He deserves to be happy with someone who actually appreciates him."

Unlike your mother, Hannah heard the unspoken words. The woman who'd abandoned him when he was seventeen, who'd chosen her own pride over her son's well-being.

Hannah reached over and squeezed Noah's hand. "He's going to love seeing you. And I can't wait to meet them both."

They finished eating in comfortable silence, and Hannah was just reaching for another wing when Noah suddenly turned to her. There was heat in his eyes now, a rekindling of the desire they'd sated in the jacuzzi.

"Hannah," he said, his voice low and rough.

She knew that tone. Knew what it meant.

Her pulse kicked up. "Yes?"

Instead of answering, Noah took the tray of food and set it on the nightstand. Then he was reaching for her, his hands finding the belt of her robe and tugging it loose. The terry cloth fell open, and his eyes darkened as he looked at her.

"Come here," he said, and it wasn't a request.

Hannah let him pull her closer, let him arrange her body beneath his. The television was still blaring weather warnings in the background, but she didn't care. All that mattered was Noah above her, Noah's hands on her skin, Noah looking at her like she was the only thing in the world that mattered.

"I've wanted this for so long," he murmured against her neck. "Wanted you for so long."

The admission made her heart soar. This was what she'd been waiting to hear: that he'd felt the same way she had, that he'd been fighting the same attraction, that all those years of careful distance had been costing him, too.

"I know," Hannah whispered, threading her fingers through his damp hair. "I've wanted you too. For so long, Noah. You have no idea."

His mouth found hers in a kiss that was slower this time, more deliberate. Less about desperate need and more about exploration, about learning each other, about savoring what they'd denied themselves for years.

Hannah sank into it, into him, letting herself feel everything she'd been holding back. The love, the desire, the hope for their future. Whatever happened after this weekend, whatever complications arose from working together, whatever fears Noah still had to overcome, they'd handle it together.

Because this was right. They were right.

And Hannah wasn't letting go.

CHAPTER 5

This time, she wanted everything different. She wanted to savor every sensation, every breath, every heartbeat between them. This wasn't just about desire anymore, it was about claiming something permanent, something real. She needed Noah to understand what had shifted between them, to recognize that she wasn't just his friend who'd fallen into his bed. She was the woman who belonged there.

The first time had been frantic, almost desperate, years of suppressed longing finally breaking free. Beautiful, yes, but too fast. Too much like they were both afraid it might never happen again. Now, in the quiet aftermath with the storm still raging outside, she wanted to prove this wasn't a fluke. Wasn't just nostalgia or convenience or the strange intimacy of being snowbound together.

This was real. This was them, finally.

She drew in a shaky breath. His scent, clean skin and something uniquely him, made her pulse skitter. How could a smell alone unravel her like this? It wasn't cologne or aftershave, just Noah. The same scent that had tortured her during movie nights on his couch, when she'd curl up beside him pretending friendship was enough. And his touch, his skin against hers, generated enough heat to chase away the blizzard howling outside their window.

"I'm hungry for you, Hannah." His lips grazed her neck, and the words rumbled through her. "You've awakened something in me. I need you again."

Her arms came around him instantly, pulling him close. The want had always been there, he'd just refused to acknowledge it. Until now. Until circumstances and courage and maybe a little bit of fate had finally broken through his stubborn walls.

"I want you too. God, Noah, I've wanted you for so long." Her voice broke on the admission, years of secret longing compressed into those few words. "Please."

"No." His mouth curved against her skin, and she could feel his smile. "This time we're going slow."

A whimper escaped before she could stop it. But she knew he was right. He'd make it everything she'd dreamed it could be, and her dreams had been detailed, frequent, and often inappropriate given their friendship. Still, the real battle, winning his heart completely, was far from over. Sex was one thing. Love was another. And she wanted both.

When his lips found hers, she melted into him, into the solid strength of his body. She pulled him closer, needing more, always more. His muscles shifted against her, and she ached to explore him, to map every plane and angle with her hands. To memorize him in case this miracle somehow slipped away.

His kiss turned fierce, demanding, and he stretched his full length against her. Every hard line of him pressed into her softness until they were tangled together, limbs entwined, breathless. His hands shaped her body to his, and she surrendered to it, to him, all thoughts of their complicated history dissolving into this moment. No more wondering if he saw her as just a friend. No more watching him date other women and pretending it didn't carve pieces from her heart.

This was what she'd wanted for years. What she'd barely let herself hope for.

His tongue swept into her mouth, and she gasped, her body arching toward his. She needed him, needed the hardness she could feel between her thighs, needed the satisfaction only Noah had ever created in her. All those years of wanting him, of hiding it behind friendship and laughter and casual touches that meant so much more to her than they did to him. And now, finally, the reality exceeded every fevered dream she'd harbored in secret.

She wanted him to fill all the empty spaces inside her. The ones that had ached for him for so long. The ones that had remained stubbornly hollow no matter who else she'd tried to let in. Because it had always been Noah. Since the day they'd met, really, though she'd spent years lying to herself about it.

Why did this feel like coming home? Like finding the place she was meant to be?

The storm raged beyond the window, wind howling and snow battering the glass in sheets of white. But another storm built between them, one she hoped would sweep her away completely. Three days, the weather channel had promised. Three days trapped in this hotel room with Noah, while the world outside became impassable. Just them, this bed, that ridiculous heart-shaped tub, and a box of condoms she'd bought with shaking hands and burning cheeks.

Everything they needed. A cocoon of time and space to figure out what came next.

His mouth moved in a trail of fire down her jaw, her neck, her shoulder. Her breathing turned harsh and uneven, every new touch wringing gasps from her throat. She threaded her fingers through his hair, loving the silky texture, the way he leaned into her touch.

"Hannah." Her name was a whisper against her skin, reverent. "I need you."

And she needed him. Desperately. Completely. In ways that terrified her because she'd already invested so much of herself in this man. If it all fell apart, if they tried and failed, if the friendship couldn't survive becoming something more, she didn't know how she'd recover.

But the risk was worth it. He was worth it.

"I'm yours," she breathed, and meant it with everything in her. She'd been his for years, he just hadn't known it. But now he'd learn the truth. Now he'd finally understand they'd been more than friends all along, at least in her heart. Every late-night conversation, every inside joke, every comfortable silence, they'd all been love letters she'd been too afraid to send.

His mouth continued its exploration, tongue lingering at the curve where her neck met her shoulder. She shivered, hypersensitive to every point of contact. Tingles cascaded through her nervous system, lighting her up like electricity. When he raised his head, his eyes captured hers, dark blue and burning with an intensity that stole her breath and made her heart stutter.

She rose to meet him as he lowered his mouth. He kissed her deeply, thoroughly, as if marking her as his. As if claiming her in a way that transcended the physical. A rightness filled her chest, sweet and aching and almost painful in its intensity. This moment belonged to them. Whatever happened tomorrow, next week, next year, right now, they were perfect together.

Then his lips found her breast, tongue circling her nipple, and coherent thought fractured. She arched into him with a cry, offering herself. Her hands fisted in his hair, holding him there, needing more, needing everything. His body molded perfectly to hers, hard muscle and heat and solid strength against her softer curves. Everywhere they touched, she burned. It was too much and not nearly enough all at once.

His hand skimmed down her ribs, over her stomach, lower.

She held her breath in anticipation. When his fingers found her center, parting her folds with deliberate care, she gasped his name like a prayer. He stroked her deliberately, expertly, clearly paying attention to every hitch in her breathing, every involuntary movement of her hips. Learning her. Reading her body's responses.

Heat spiraled through her core, building with each caress. She gripped the sheets, knuckles white, sensation building in waves that grew higher and higher. Her hips moved in rhythm with his hand, seeking more pressure, more friction, more of everything he was giving her.

"That's it," he murmured against her ear, his voice rough. "Let go for me."

And she did. The tension coiled impossibly tight and then released all at once, pleasure crashing through her in waves that left her gasping and shaking. She cried out, not caring how desperate she sounded, how thoroughly undone. This was Noah. She could be vulnerable with him. She could be real.

She lay trembling in the aftermath, heart racing against her ribs like it might break free. She clung to his shoulders, needing the anchor of his solid presence. He kissed her temple, her eyelids, her nose, tender touches while she caught her breath and reassembled herself. She could feel him hard against her thigh, patient but ready, waiting for her.

The consideration in that waiting, the way he put her pleasure first, made her chest ache with something deeper than desire.

"Hannah." His voice was rough with need, strained with holding back. "Love me."

The words stunned her, even though she knew he probably meant the physical act. But what if he meant more? What if, somewhere in the tangle of friendship and want and this storm-forced proximity, he was starting to feel what she'd felt for years?

Don't get ahead of yourself, she thought. But hope bloomed anyway, stubborn and bright.

Right now, it didn't matter. She'd give him anything. Everything.

She reached between them and wrapped her fingers around him, stroking slowly from base to tip. His face contorted with pleasure, jaw clenching, and a groan tore from his throat that went straight to her core.

"God, Hannah. Don't stop."

She didn't. She explored him with growing confidence, learning what made him gasp, what made his hips jerk involuntarily. Power surged through her. This man, her best friend, the person who knew her better than anyone, craved her touch. Wanted her. Maybe even needed her in ways that went beyond the physical.

The knowledge thrilled and terrified her in equal measure. She couldn't lose him. Not as a friend, and not as this, whatever this was becoming.

She drew her palm over the sensitive tip, and his hand shot out, grabbing her wrist. His breathing was ragged, control visibly fraying. When his eyes met hers, they blazed with barely restrained hunger.

She cupped his face with her free hand and pulled him down for a kiss, pouring everything she felt into it. All the years of secret longing. All the hope for what they might become. All the love she'd carried silently for so long.

"This time we're using a condom," he gasped, moving to the side of the bed.

"In the drawer."

He shot her a look, somewhere between surprise and understanding that she'd planned this, that she'd hoped for this possibility even before they'd left for this trip. His expression was unreadable for a moment, and her heart seized with sudden fear. Was he upset? Did he think she'd manipulated him?

But then he yanked the drawer open without comment, and relief flooded through her. Within seconds, he'd found the box, torn open a packet, and sheathed himself with practiced efficiency. When he returned to her, his eyes had darkened to midnight blue, pupils blown wide with want.

"Make love to me," she whispered, the words intimate and vulnerable.

His mouth claimed hers with urgent hunger, and she opened to him completely. She guided him home with a trembling hand, lifting her hips to meet his. When he entered her, slow and deep, she welcomed him with her whole body. A soft sound escaped her, relief and pleasure and rightness all tangled together.

She'd never tire of this. Of him filling her so completely, of being connected to him in this most intimate way. It felt like pieces of a puzzle finally clicking into place.

He moved inside her with a rhythm that started slow but gradually built. Each thrust deliberate, measured, driving her steadily toward the edge. She wrapped her legs around his waist, changing the angle, taking him deeper. Perfect. God, it was perfect.

With every stroke, she matched him, met him, lifted her hips to draw him in further. She felt her heart reaching for his, yearning for an emotional connection to match the physical one. Pleasure sparked low in her belly and caught fire, burning hotter and brighter with each movement.

His forehead pressed against hers, their breath mingling. She could see every flicker of emotion in his eyes, desire, yes, but also something softer. Something that looked almost like wonder.

"Noah." His name tore from her throat as the tension coiled impossibly tight. She was so close, teetering on the edge. "Please."

"I've got you," he murmured, and somehow those simple words undid her completely.

She looked up into his eyes, needing that connection, that final piece, and the world exploded. Pleasure detonated through her in waves that seemed endless, radiating out from her core to every nerve ending. She cried out, clutching him, lost in sensation so intense it bordered on overwhelming.

He followed her over the edge with a shuddered groan, her name on his lips. They collapsed together, breathless and slick with sweat, hearts pounding in tandem. For a long moment, neither of them moved. She felt shattered in the best possible way, remade into something new. Something that included him in ways that went bone-deep.

The television cast a flickering blue light across them. Outside, the storm continued its assault on the windows. But here, in their cocoon of rumpled sheets and shared breath, everything felt safe. Right.

After a long, comfortable silence, she laughed softly against his shoulder. "I think we need to eat. I'm still starving."

He chuckled, the sound rumbling through his chest where it pressed against hers. He rolled toward her, propping himself on one elbow, and brushed a strand of hair from her face with unexpected tenderness. "That didn't satisfy you?"

"Completely," she assured him, tracing her fingers along his jaw, loving the slight scrape of stubble. "But before we do that again, and we are definitely doing that again, I need sustenance." She stretched lazily, feeling pleasantly used and utterly content. "That was incredible, by the way. Even better than the first time."

He grinned, looking impossibly smug and adorable at once. The combination shouldn't work, but on him it did. "I aim to please."

"Mission accomplished." She traced idle patterns on his chest, reluctant to break the spell of this moment. "Now, where are those chicken wings? Because I'm pretty sure we're going to need our strength."

His laugh was warm and genuine. "Three-day blizzard, remember?"

"Exactly." She smiled up at him, hope and happiness and cautious optimism swelling in her chest. "Three whole days."

Three days to convince him this could work. Three days to show him they could be more than friends without losing what made them friends. Three days to make him fall in love with her, or at least start down that path.

The storm outside could keep the world at bay. And in here, they could figure out what came next.

Together.

CHAPTER 6

*L*ater that night, Noah lay with Hannah curled beside him, her warmth seeping into his side as he listened to the wind howl outside like some predator trying to claw its way in. Ice pellets struck the windows in irregular bursts, and the panes rattled in their frames with each gust. The storm showed no signs of letting up.

What the hell was he doing? Had he completely lost his mind?

They were friends. Best friends. The kind of friendship that had sustained him through his worst days in the ER, through failed relationships, through the grinding exhaustion of residency. He didn't want to lose her, couldn't imagine his life without her in it, but tonight had been the best sex of his life. It was like they fit together perfectly, like two puzzle pieces he'd never realized belonged together. Like they were made for one another.

And that terrified him.

His stomach twisted at the memory of that first time earlier. The urgency, the desperate need, the way they'd fallen into each other without thinking. They hadn't used a condom. Jesus. What if she were pregnant? The thought sent his heart racing for all the wrong reasons. That would change everything, wouldn't it? Sure, he wanted children someday, but with his wife, not with his best friend, whom he'd accidentally gotten pregnant in a moment of passion.

Although lying here with her soft breath warming his chest, he couldn't help wondering if maybe she was the right one. The only one who'd ever felt right, if he was honest with himself.

No other woman he'd met had understood him the way Hannah did. No one else could read his moods after a brutal shift, knowing when to offer comfort and when to just sit in silence with him. No one else made him laugh the way she did, or challenged him, or made him want to be better. And God knew he'd tried to find someone else. He'd dated plenty over the years, always half-hoping one of them would stick, would give him a reason to stop thinking about Hannah as anything more than a friend.

None of them ever had.

The memory of his adoptive parents screaming at one another slammed into his consciousness like a physical blow. Almost every night when they came home from work, the fighting would start. His mother would disagree with how his father had treated a patient. His father would tell her she was so stupid he didn't know how she'd made it through medical school. On and on and on they would fight, their voices rising, filling the house with venom until finally one of them would storm off to the bedroom and slam the door hard enough to rattle the pictures on the walls.

Every single night, from the time he was five years old until the day his mother finally said enough and left, they did this.

He'd learned early that it was best if he stayed in his bedroom with the door closed and his hands pressed over his ears. Some-times he'd turn on music, anything to drown out the sound of people who were supposed to love each other, tearing each other apart.

And still, somehow, he'd wanted to become a doctor.

After listening to their stories, the ones they'd share during the brief peaceful moments, usually at breakfast before the day's resentments built up, their successes and their failures, he'd wanted to be part of this profession that treated the human body. Medicine was so interesting, the human body so intriguing. The way everything worked together in perfect harmony until suddenly it didn't, and then it was his job to figure out why and fix it.

He loved being a doctor. Loved healing people, saving lives, making a difference. But sometimes he thought he would do better in another field of medicine, something slower, more methodical. Something where he didn't have to watch children die.

The ER was fast-paced, and some nights were absolutely brutal. The kids got to him every single time. You weren't human if you weren't affected by a child hurt in a car accident or a drive-by shooting. And the abuse cases, parents beating their own kids, those he would never understand. How could you hurt something so small and helpless, something that depended on you for everything?

But the work was always interesting, never boring. That much he'd inherited from his parents, that love of medicine that transcended their toxic marriage.

Could he and Hannah work together without screaming at one another? Without letting the stress, pressure, and life-and-death decisions corrode what they had? His children, if he ever had children, would never have to listen to their parents yelling the way he had growing up. His children would not hear their parents call each other names or scream that the other was stupid or watch one throw a drink at the other's head.

Before that ever happened, he would pick them up and leave. Pack a bag in the middle of the night and go. But the best plan of action was to make certain the person you married was not going to turn out half-crazy. And his mother had serious mental issues, bipolar, he'd realized later, though it had never been officially diagnosed, while his father did his best to keep her happy until she came after him verbally. Then the fight was on, and there was no stopping it until someone retreated.

It was a roller coaster life he refused to get back on.

Thank God they had never turned on him. They'd loved him in their own way, he supposed. From the time he was five years old, he'd listened to their arguments, learned to read the signs of when things were about to escalate. By the time he was a teenager, he couldn't wait to get out of that house, to escape to college and never look back.

Sure, he and Hannah had disagreements. They were human beings with different opinions, different approaches to problems. But they had never yelled at one another. Never called each other names or tried to wound with their words. Their arguments were more like spirited debates that usually ended in laughter or compromise.

But could they work together all day in the pressure cooker of the ER, come home at night, and not drag each other through the mud? Not start questioning each other's medical decisions, second-guessing each other's judgment calls? Medicine had destroyed his parents' marriage. What made him think it wouldn't destroy his relationship with Hannah?

Occasionally, they drank champagne to celebrate, a successful difficult intubation, a patient who beat the odds, a particularly good day. But would one or both of them eventually reach a point where they'd toss a martini at the other one over some disagreement about treatment protocol? No. He refused to live that life again. That chapter was over.

This fear was exactly why he'd never pursued Hannah romantically, why he'd kept his attraction carefully locked away. The woman was gorgeous, her blonde hair that caught the light like spun gold, those emerald eyes that seemed to see straight through him, the way her full lips would curve into a smile that made his heart stutter. And her body, God, her body was curvaceous and full and so tempting he'd spent years trying not to notice.

They seemed to fit together perfectly. Just the smell of her, something floral and clean with a hint of vanilla, aroused him in ways he'd tried hard to ignore.

With a sigh, he rolled toward her and put his arm around her, pulling her closer. He breathed in her fresh scent and felt his cock begin to harden once again. Apparently, his body had no interest in his mental conflicts and reservations.

Asleep, she moaned softly but snuggled up against him, her body instinctively seeking his warmth. Unless he wanted to wake her, and he definitely wanted to wake her, he should probably get out of bed and give himself some space to think clearly.

Rising carefully so as not to disturb her, he walked naked to the window and gazed out at the snow. It was still coming down in thick, heavy flakes, illuminated by the hotel's exterior lights. The parking lot was completely buried, cars reduced to white lumps. They weren't going anywhere tomorrow. Maybe not for days.

What if he'd screwed his friendship up? What if this ruined everything?

Turning from the window, he gazed at Hannah curled on her side, sleeping peacefully with her arm tucked beneath her head. A beautiful picture of innocence and trust, completely vulnerable in sleep. His chest tightened with something he was afraid to name.

Maybe it was a mistake, but it was the best mistake he'd made in a long time. Hell, maybe ever.

He'd found no one he wanted to spend the rest of his life with, had almost resigned himself to perpetual bachelorhood. But he couldn't imagine a day without Hannah, laughing at him, poking fun at his terrible coffee brewing skills, talking to him about his patients, easing his pain when he lost someone on the table. There was so much they shared, so much history and understanding between them. Tonight made perfect sense in ways that scared him.

But the pain of listening to his parents screaming at one another was still there, a painful reminder of everything that could go wrong. Was he willing to risk his friendship with Hannah, the peaceful life he'd carefully constructed, to take a chance on something more?

He wasn't certain. And that uncertainty felt like cowardice.

With a soft sigh, she rolled over in her sleep, and her hand searched the bed for him, patting the empty space where he'd been.

"Noah," she murmured sleepily, a small frown creasing her forehead.

"I'm right here," he said, his voice rough as he walked back to the bed. "I wanted to see if it was still snowing."

"Is it?" Her eyes remained closed, voice thick with sleep.

"Yes," he said, crawling back under the covers with her, immediately feeling more settled just being close to her again.

She shivered as his cooler skin touched hers. "I'm cold. Warm me up."

Oh, if he touched her the way he wanted to, he would be doing a hell of a lot more than just sharing body heat with her.

Pulling her tightly against him, his cock nudged insistently between her legs. Even half-asleep, her body responded to his, pressing back against him.

"Hmm," she said dreamily, her lips curving into a small smile. "You're hard again."

"You do that to me," he admitted, being completely truthful.

He was in so much trouble. How could he walk away from Hannah after this? How could they just go back to being friends after what they'd shared? How was he supposed to pretend his world hadn't just shifted on its axis?

A smile spread across her face, and she arched back against him deliberately. "We can sleep in tomorrow. No rounds. No having to wait for the next ambulance to arrive. No traumas. Just us."

"Yes," he said, nuzzling her neck, breathing in her scent. She smelled so damn good, like home and desire all mixed together.

Rolling toward him, she opened her eyes fully, and in the dim light from outside, he could see they were bright with want. "I never thought it would be this good between us."

"Me either," he admitted, his hand trailing down her side. "But I'm glad it is."

"Me too," she said, her hand finding his hip, pulling him closer. "Now get busy. Dawn is three hours away, but we can sleep in after."

"Yes, we can," he replied, his mouth already descending toward hers.

Thank God she'd found them this hotel room. He didn't know what they would have done if they'd gotten stuck in the car or, worse, separated by the storm. This bubble of time felt like a gift, a chance to figure out what the hell they were doing before the real world intruded.

His mouth covered hers, and she moaned into the kiss, her body already moving against his with familiar urgency.

Suddenly, she released his lips, her hand pressing against his chest.

"Don't forget the condom," she said firmly, her eyes serious despite the desire written all over her face.

"I won't," he promised. He'd learned his lesson. "Now let me do my job."

"Gladly," she replied, pulling him back down to her.

And as he lost himself in her again, the doubts and fears receded, at least for now. Tomorrow he could worry about what this meant, about whether they were making a mistake, about whether love was worth the risk.

Tonight, he just wanted Hannah.

CHAPTER 7

The next morning, when Hannah woke, she stretched luxuriously in the king-size bed and couldn't suppress the grin that spread across her face. Last night had been wonderful. Better than she'd dreamed possible, and she'd spent years dreaming about what it would be like to be with Noah.

The reality had exceeded every fantasy.

Her body felt deliciously used, pleasantly sore in ways that made heat bloom in her cheeks. She could still feel the ghost of his hands on her skin, the press of his mouth against hers, the way he'd looked at her in those unguarded moments when passion stripped away all his usual caution.

Jumping up from bed with an energy that surprised her given how little sleep they'd gotten, she ran naked to the window. The cool air raised goosebumps on her bare skin as she peeked through the heavy curtains and laughed out loud. It was still snowing, if anything, almost as hard as yesterday. Fat flakes swirled in the wind, and she could barely make out the shapes of buried cars in the parking lot below.

They would not be going anywhere today. Maybe not tomorrow either.

The thought filled her with a giddy relief she tried not to examine too closely. More time. More chances to show Noah this could work between them. More opportunities to convince him to take a risk on them.

Running back to the bed, she bounced on it like a kid on Christmas morning. "Get up, sleepyhead. It's still snowing!"

A groan emanated from the lump of blankets and pillows that was Noah. One muscular arm emerged to cover his face. "Why are we waking up so early?"

"Because I'm starving," she said, continuing to bounce until the mattress jostled him. "I want to go downstairs to the restaurant and eat a huge breakfast, and then I want to go outside and play in the snow. Build a snowman. Have a snowball fight. Besides, it's after nine."

That was late for her normally. Years of medical training had turned her into an early riser who could function on minimal sleep. But last night they'd stayed awake into the small hours making love, talking softly in the darkness, learning each other's bodies in ways that still made her pulse quicken. And she didn't regret a single moment. The night had been beautiful between them, tender and passionate and perfect in ways she'd barely let herself hope for.

He finally lowered his arm and squinted at her, his dark hair adorably rumpled. "Are you ten years old?"

She laughed, delighted by his teasing tone. "Yes, I am still that ten-year-old who used to build a snowman whenever we had snow in Oklahoma."

They'd often had snow in her little town, and the memories rushed back warm and bright, building snowmen with her brothers and sisters, making snow ice cream with vanilla and sugar, having epic snowball fights that ended with everyone soaked and laughing. Her parents still lived in that same house, in that same small town, though she hadn't been home to see them in four months.

Too long. Way too long.

Her family was normal and loving, and she missed them with a sudden, sharp ache. But they all had busy lives now. Her mother was a nurse in Oklahoma City, working long shifts in the ICU, and she'd encouraged Hannah for years to become a doctor. "You're smart enough," she'd say. "And you have the heart for it."

Thankfully, Hannah had followed her advice, and she loved working in the ER. The fast-paced environment made the time pass quickly, kept her sharp and focused. And the cases she saw were often diverse, tragic, heartbreaking, and occasionally miraculous. Every shift was different. Every patient mattered.

"I'm naked and I'm going to get in the shower," she announced, climbing off the bed with deliberate sensuality. She let her voice drop lower, teasing. "I'm going to wash my body and I'll be all clean and wet."

Noah opened one eye fully, his gaze tracking over her bare skin with an intensity that made her feel powerful and desired. "Damn, woman, you know how to tempt a man. Why did I not know about this side of you?"

She grinned and swung her hips as she walked to the bathroom, very aware of his eyes on her. He hadn't known because he'd never let himself look. Because he'd been too scared to see what had been right in front of him for years.

But he was looking now. And she intended to make sure he kept looking.

A few minutes later, she'd turned on the shower and was testing the water temperature when she heard him pad into the bathroom.

"Anyone in here need some help scrubbing?" His voice was rough with sleep and something else that made her stomach flip.

This was the Noah she loved, the playful, fun guy who emerged when he let his guard down. Not the serious, controlled doctor who kept everyone at arm's length.

"Oh, I think my back needs to be washed," she said innocently, glancing over her shoulder at him.

He stepped into the shower behind her, and the space suddenly felt smaller, more intimate. Picking up the washcloth, he started working on her back with slow, deliberate strokes. She leaned back against his chest, feeling the solid warmth of him, the way his heart beat steady and strong against her spine.

Turning her head, she kissed him, her mouth covering his as steam rose around them. When they broke apart, both breathing harder, she sighed with contentment.

"I really enjoyed last night."

"Me too," he said, and she heard something in his voice, surprise maybe, or wonder. As if he hadn't expected it to be this good either.

"But this morning, we need to eat a good meal," she continued, trying to keep things light even as her heart hammered with hope. "And then someone I know wants to play in the snow."

He chuckled, the sound rumbling through his chest. "I wonder if the hotel has an area where we can go, or if there's a park nearby."

Taking the washcloth from him, she soaped it up and washed his back, her hands moving over the muscles she'd explored so thoroughly in the darkness. When he turned around, she saw he was hard for her again, and heat pooled low in her belly.

"Doctor Baker," she said in her most professional voice, even as her lips twitched with amusement. "You seem to have this growth protruding from between your legs. Let me examine that, and then we'll need to consider surgery."

He pulled her up against him, and she could feel every hard line of his body pressed to her softer curves. He kissed her hard on the mouth, hungry and demanding. "I need food before we can do this again."

"Thank God," she said dramatically, pressing her hand to her forehead. "I feared I would faint from hunger."

Stepping out of the shower before she lost her resolve, because she absolutely could be persuaded to skip breakfast, she left him alone as she quickly toweled off and went in search of clothes. If they were going outside, she wanted to dress as warmly as possible. Jeans, thermal underwear, a thick sweater, wool socks.

A few minutes later, she heard the hair dryer blowing and knew he was almost ready. Years ago, she'd given up wearing much makeup. It was always a concern in the operating room, you didn't want mascara running into your eyes during a twelve-hour surgery. So she only wore it on special occasions now.

Today felt like one of those times. Today felt significant, like the beginning of something that could change everything.

She quickly applied a little concealer and powder, some mascara to make her eyes pop, a touch of lip gloss. Nothing dramatic, just enough to feel put together and pretty.

When Noah walked out of the bathroom, fully dressed and looking unfairly handsome with his damp hair and that small smile playing at his lips, she was ready.

"Let's go eat," he said, offering his hand.

"Yes," she replied, lacing her fingers through his.

The simple gesture felt momentous. They were holding hands. Walking out of their room together like a couple, not just friends.

They walked out of the honeymoon suite, and an older couple was waiting at the elevator. The man had silver hair and kind eyes, and the woman wore a wedding ring that looked worn smooth from decades of wear.

"Congratulations, you two," the woman said with a warm smile. "We've been married for forty years."

Hannah's breath caught. Forty years. Forty years of waking up next to the same person, of building a life together, of choosing each other over and over again.

"No, you're the ones who we should be congratulating," Noah said easily. "Forty years is incredible. We're just getting started."

Hannah's heart leaped in her chest so hard she almost gasped. Did he really mean that, or was he just playing along for appearances? This was exactly what she wanted, to be the kind of couple who made it to forty years, who weathered storms together and came out stronger.

In forty years, she wanted to be standing in an elevator telling another young couple about their journey together.

The elevator arrived and they all stepped on. The older man pushed the button for the lobby.

"Can you believe this weather?" the woman asked, shaking her head.

"Incredible," Hannah agreed, trying to calm her racing heart. "We don't get anything like this in Texas."

The couple laughed. "I guess not," the man replied. "This is unusual even for Montana. Haven't seen a storm like this in probably twenty years."

When they reached the ground floor, people milled about the lobby—families with restless children, couples holding coffee cups, a few business travelers looking frustrated as they talked on cell phones. The restaurant was doing steady business, and they put their names on the waiting list.

The older couple waved goodbye and disappeared into the hotel gift shop, their heads bent together in conversation, still connected after all these years.

"Forty years," Noah said, watching them go. His voice had gone flat, distant. "My parents would have killed each other if they'd stayed married that long."

The words hit her like cold water. She'd almost forgotten that his parents had divorced when he was young, forgotten because he never really talked about them. Never shared much about that part of his life, and she'd learned not to push.

But maybe she needed to push now. Maybe understanding

where he came from was the key to showing him they could have a different future.

When they were alone later, she needed to ask him about that time in his life. About what it had been like growing up in a house full of anger and resentment. She'd met him in medical school in a study group, he'd been brilliant and driven and charming in small doses, keeping everyone at a friendly distance.

It had taken her months to work her way past his defenses enough to be called a friend.

At graduation, she'd met his father, but at the time, the older man had been living in Houston. Now he'd returned to his hometown of Whitefish, Montana, and remarried. That was the reason they were here, to meet his new stepmother, to see if his father had finally found happiness.

The hostess called Noah's name, and they hurried into the restaurant. She led them to a table by the big glass windows that lined one wall. Outside, the patio area was buried under at least four feet of snow, drifts piled higher against the building.

"We could play on the patio," Hannah said, her earlier enthusiasm returning. "I bet we could make snow tunnels. Snow forts."

"You're crazy," Noah said, but he was laughing. "We could take the jeep out and test it in the snow. I've never driven in the stuff. Might be good for me to practice before we get out on the highway."

"Did you check to see if the highways were open this morning?" she asked, even though she secretly hoped they weren't.

"Not with the snow still coming down like it is," he said. "But I can check later."

Her brows raised hopefully. "We could take the jeep out and let you practice. That way you'd be more prepared when we eventually drive to Whitefish."

"If we get to go," he said, and she couldn't tell if he was relieved or disappointed by the delay.

The waitress hurried over to their table.

"Coffee?" the young woman asked, looking harried.

"Yes, please," Hannah said gratefully, then turned back to Noah. "Was your father all right with us not arriving for a couple of days?"

He nodded. "He said he understood. The storm's hitting Whitefish even harder than here. He told us to let him know when we could leave safely."

Hannah wrapped her hands around the warm coffee mug when it arrived, letting the heat seep into her palms. "Do you know anything about your birth father and mother?"

The question had been hovering in her mind for years, but she'd never quite had the courage to ask. Now, in the intimacy of everything they'd shared, it felt like the right time.

"Not really," he said, his expression closing down slightly. "I know my adoptive mother didn't want to talk about them. She said they were my parents and that's all I needed to know."

Hannah's heart ached for the boy he must have been, trying to understand where he came from, who he looked like, why he'd been given up. She couldn't imagine not knowing anything about her origins. Sure, he'd had his adoptive parents, but from what little he'd shared, that didn't seem to have been the best environment to raise a child.

What would his life have been like with his birth mother and father from the very beginning? Would he be different, more open, less guarded? Or would he be the same man sitting across from her now, the one she'd fallen in love with despite all his walls?

"Do you regret that you weren't raised by your real mother?" she asked softly.

He shrugged, but she saw the tension in his shoulders. "My adoptive parents loved me. I never doubted that. They just hated each other. As for my birth mother and father, I don't know anything about them. Not everyone had a wonderful family growing up like you did."

The words stung a little, not because he meant them to, but because she heard the pain underneath. The longing for something he'd never had.

That was true. She'd been lucky to grow up in a house full of laughter and love, where her parents still held hands after thirty years of marriage, where family dinners were loud and chaotic and wonderful. And she wanted to give her own children someday that same safe, warm, loving home.

She hoped that Noah would be a good, capable father. But sometimes people who were raised in bad environments recreated what they grew up with, unable to break the cycle. That was a concern that gnawed at her in quiet moments.

Could he be different? Would he be different?

The waitress walked back over, interrupting her thoughts. "Folks, we've got eggs and pancakes. That's about it. Storm's delayed our food delivery."

"I'll take two eggs over medium with a side of hash browns," Hannah said, realizing how hungry she actually was.

"I'll take the same," Noah said, and the waitress turned and walked off.

"You don't think they'll run out of food, do you?" Hannah asked, gazing at Noah with sudden concern. "Maybe we should take the jeep out after breakfast and see if we can find a grocery store that's open. Stock up just in case."

"Good idea," he agreed.

"Besides, that will keep us out of bed for a little while," she added with a grin, trying to lighten the mood.

Noah tilted his head and stared at her, his expression going serious in a way that made her stomach tighten. "How is this going to work between us? We're in uncharted territory and I'm nervous."

There it was. The doubt she'd seen flickering in his eyes, the fear that had kept them apart for so long.

She reached out and took his hand, brought it to her lips, and pressed a kiss to his knuckles. "We are in uncharted territory," she agreed quietly. "But it's what I've been wanting for a long time, Noah. A long time."

For a moment, she stared at him, waiting, hoping he would say the words she needed to hear. That he wanted this too. That he was willing to try, to risk his heart, to believe they could be different from his parents.

But instead, he glanced away, his jaw tightening.

Oh, there were still doubts there. She could see them in his eyes, in the set of his shoulders, in the way he couldn't quite meet her gaze. And it hurt more than she wanted to admit.

But it was now or never as far as she was concerned. She wasn't going to wait forever for this man to get over his fears. He needed to make up his mind and soon.

When they'd finished their residency, her family had begged her to come home to Oklahoma. Her mother had even helped her line up interviews at hospitals in Oklahoma City and Tulsa. But she hadn't wanted to leave Noah. She'd stayed in Texas, taken the ER position, built her life around the hope that someday he would see what was right in front of him.

But now, after this weekend, after everything they'd shared, if things didn't go as she hoped, she would pack up and leave. She'd go home to Oklahoma, where her family wanted her, where she could build a life without constantly waiting for Noah to be ready.

Her family wanted her even if Noah didn't.

The thought brought tears to her eyes that she blinked away furiously. She wouldn't cry. Not here, not now. She'd give this weekend everything she had, show him what they could be together.

And if he still couldn't see it, couldn't take the leap, then at least she'd know she tried.

At least she'd have these memories of what might have been.

CHAPTER 8

$\mathcal{A}$n hour later, they were outside, bundled up, and cleaning off the jeep. Snow continued to fall, and the wind blew the stinging flakes into his face, each one a tiny needle of ice against his skin. Thank goodness the rental car company had included a brush to wipe the snow off the windows and the roof. Even so, with the rate at which the snow was falling, it wouldn't be long before the windows were covered once again.

Noah had started the vehicle to warm it up and then stepped back out into the cold, his breath forming white clouds in the frigid air. The temperature had to be hovering somewhere around fifteen degrees, maybe colder with the wind chill. He wasn't used to this kind of cold, Texas winters were laughable compared to this Montana deep freeze. His fingers were already going numb inside his gloves as he scraped at the ice forming beneath the snow on the windshield.

As he stood by the jeep door, working methodically to clear the driver's side, a snowball came hurling toward him. He ducked just in time, feeling it whiz past his ear.

"Hey, I'm working here," he hollered, unable to keep the grin off his face even as he tried to sound stern.

"And I'm playing," Hannah replied, her laughter carrying across the parking lot like music.

There was a spirited side of Hannah that always lightened the mood, even in the hospital during their worst shifts. It was one of the things he admired most about her, no, if he was being honest with himself, one of the things he loved about her. How easily she could become fun and playful, and then in the blink of an eye, transform into a serious, focused medical professional. She never lost herself in either role. She was fully present in every moment, whether she was throwing snowballs or saving lives.

It was a quality his mother had never possessed. His mother had always been so consumed by her work, so driven by her ambition, that there had been no room for lightness, no space for joy. Every dinner conversation had turned into a medical debate with his father. Every family outing had been cut short by an emergency page. Every birthday party interrupted by a phone call that couldn't wait.

But Hannah was different. Hannah knew how to live.

Grabbing snow from around his knees, Noah balled it up and threw it back at her, putting more force behind it than he'd intended. She dodged it easily, already prepared with a stockpile of perfectly formed snowballs lined up on the hood of a nearby car.

She bombarded him, hitting him square in the chest with three rapid-fire throws. The woman had an arm on her, he'd have to remember that.

Sneaking around the side of the jeep, using it as cover, Noah came up behind her and picked her up, wrapping his arms around her waist and lifting her off the ground. She squealed, her legs kicking playfully as she tried to twist around to face him.

Right now, he'd love to throw her into the snow and have his way with her right out here in this empty parking lot, consequences be damned. But there was the very real danger of frostbite to certain areas of his anatomy he wasn't willing to risk. Not to mention the fact that they were both already shivering despite their winter gear.

"It's time you got in the jeep," he said, but he didn't put her down immediately. Instead, he held her there, enjoying the way she smelled of some lotion she always wore, something vanilla and warm, something that reminded him of comfort and home even though he'd never really had a home that felt like either of those things. The scent had him nuzzling her neck, his cold nose against her warm skin making her laugh and squirm in his arms.

She turned in his arms, and for a moment, they stood holding one another while snowflakes bombarded them from above. The world around them seemed to disappear, the cold, the wind, the snow, all of it faded into the background. All Noah could feel was the warmth of her body against his, reminding him just how cold he'd been before she snuggled close. Her arms wrapped around his neck, and she looked up at him with those eyes that saw right through every wall he'd ever built.

This was dangerous territory. This feeling expanding in his chest, this warmth that had nothing to do with body heat and everything to do with the way she fit against him. This was just a weekend thing. Just two colleagues letting off steam, enjoying each other's company with no strings attached. No complications. No expectations.

So why did it feel like so much more?

"Where are we going?" Hannah asked, breaking the spell, though she didn't pull away from him.

"The desk clerk told me there was a park not far from the grocery store. I thought we'd go to the market first and get what we want, and then we could go to the park and build a snowman."

The woman's smile lit up her entire face, transforming her from beautiful to radiant, and she actually danced in his arms, bouncing on her toes like a child on Christmas morning.

"Let's go!" she exclaimed.

They both piled into the jeep and Noah took a deep breath,

his hands gripping the steering wheel perhaps a bit too tightly. He'd never driven in snow before. Never had to. All he wanted was to get them back to the hotel without wrecking the vehicle, or worse, hurting Hannah. The thought of her getting injured because of his inexperience made his stomach clench with anxiety.

"Put it in four-wheel drive," Hannah said, apparently sensing his nervousness. "The snow is so deep, we're going to need all four wheels to go anywhere."

He found the lever, grateful for her guidance, but waited until they were going ten miles an hour before pulling down the switch from two wheels to four. That was what the attendant at the car rental place had told him, drilling the instruction into his head with the kind of repetition usually reserved for teaching medical students how to intubate. He'd known he would need to use the four-wheel-drive function when they drove, but knowing it and doing it were two different things.

Immediately, he felt the difference in how the vehicle responded, felt the tires gripping the snow-covered pavement better, and he was more certain they were not going to get stuck, though he still maintained his white-knuckled grip on the wheel.

Hannah had looked up the closest grocery store on her phone, her face illuminated by the screen's glow in the grey afternoon light.

"Turn right out of the parking lot, and then we're going about a mile down this road, and you'll need to make a left turn."

There were very few cars on the road, and Noah couldn't help but think about what the emergency room and emergency services in town must be going through right now with this storm. It would be a busy, chaotic time with accidents, slips and falls, heart attacks, and all the other traumas and emergencies normally dealt with during severe weather. He'd worked enough bad storms in Houston to know the pattern.

It seemed that there were more attempted suicides during the holidays than usual, too. Those were always the worst cases for Noah, the ones that haunted him long after his shift ended. Not only because you knew someone hated their life enough to try to end it, but because of his own family situation, because of what had happened with his mother.

And here they were, out acting like all the crazies they saw in the ER, driving in a snowstorm instead of staying safely at the hotel where any sane person would be. But Noah had needed to get out of that room for a little while, needed the change of scenery, needed something to break the spell of intimacy that was starting to feel too real, too permanent. If they stayed cooped up in that hotel room much longer, they would find themselves in bed together again, and Noah wasn't sure he could keep pretending this was just casual if they crossed that line one more time.

Glancing into the mirrors, side and rearview, checking his blind spots even though there was barely any traffic, Noah moved into the left lane and came to the stoplight. He pressed the brake pedal, and his heart lurched when the brakes were slow to respond, the vehicle sliding slightly on the packed snow beneath them. He wasn't going that fast, maybe twenty miles an hour, but it felt like an eternity before they finally came to a halt, stopping several feet short of the intersection.

The car going in the opposite direction wasn't so lucky, or perhaps wasn't so cautious. Noah watched in horror as the sedan slid right through the intersection, the driver clearly pumping the brakes but getting no response, the vehicle hydroplaning on the ice beneath the snow. Thank goodness no other cars were coming through the cross street, or they would have witnessed a serious collision.

"And that's why the ER is probably full today," Hannah said quietly, and Noah heard the professional assessment in her voice, the same tone she used when they were standing in the trauma bay waiting for an incoming ambulance.

"Yes," he replied, thinking back to when they had worked through Hurricane Harvey, that nightmare shift that had seemed to last forty-eight hours straight. It seemed there had been more heart attacks that night than he ever remembered seeing in such a concentrated time frame. Maybe it was the stress of the storm, the anxiety of not knowing if your home would still be standing when you finally got to go check on it. Or maybe it was people doing stupid things they wouldn't normally do, like putting off taking their medications or overexerting themselves trying to prepare for the worst.

The light changed to green, but Noah waited, looking carefully in all directions to make certain everyone was stopped, that no one else was sliding through intersections, before he gently pressed the accelerator and moved cautiously through the intersection.

They made it through safely, and Noah saw the grocery store not far away, its lights bright against the grey-white landscape. When he pulled into the parking lot, being extra careful with his turns and his speed, Hannah turned and smiled at him with genuine warmth.

"Good job," she said. "Now let's go grab some munchies."

When they walked into the store, Noah was amazed at what he saw. There were two cashiers busy checking people out, working at a frantic pace, but the shelves were almost completely bare, like something out of a post-apocalyptic movie. Empty spaces gaped where products should have been, and what little remained looked picked over and sad.

"What the hell?" Noah said, stopping in his tracks to stare at the devastation.

"Trucks can't get into town," a man said, pushing past them with his own nearly-empty cart. "And people knew the storm was coming, so they stocked up. Should have been here yesterday."

"Thanks," Hannah said as they walked through the store, surveying the damage. "Hope you didn't want anything special."

"I'd just like some dip and chips and maybe some lunch meat," Noah said, trying to keep his expectations low. "That way, if the restaurant runs out of food, we'd have something to fall back on."

"I want some fruit," Hannah replied. "But that's not looking too good."

She wasn't wrong. The produce section looked like it had been ransacked. The bananas were completely gone, not even any brown ones left behind. There were some apples, slightly bruised, a couple containers of blueberries, and a few oranges that had definitely seen better days. Hannah picked through them carefully, selecting the best of what remained.

They went through the store systematically, managing to find some crackers, a jar of salsa, a package of cheddar cheese that hadn't been claimed, and some deli turkey that was close to its sell-by date but would probably be fine for another day or two. By the time they reached the checkout, their cart had maybe ten items in it, and Noah felt oddly proud that they'd managed to find even that much.

Hannah pulled out her credit card before Noah could reach for his wallet.

"I was going to get the groceries," he protested, even though he knew it was a losing battle. Hannah was fiercely independent, had been since the day he met her.

"You rented the Jeep and I'm so glad you did," she replied, handing her card to the cashier. "Besides, you're taking me to the park where we can build a snowman."

Shaking his head, Noah glanced at her, unable to stop the smile that tugged at his lips. "You really are ten years old."

"Why not?" Hannah challenged, her eyes sparkling with mischief. "What else are we going to do? Go back to the hotel and..." A grin spread across her face and Noah laughed despite himself. She had a point. A very good point.

"I brought a medical book I'm reading," he said, trying to

sound virtuous and failing miserably. "That new cardiothoracic surgery text that just came out."

"Well, good for you," Hannah said with mock seriousness. "I'm on vacation and I brought a juicy, sexy romance novel that is going to make me so ready for you."

They reached the cashier and the young woman gazed at them with a mixture of amusement and something that might have been pity.

"You're from out of town?" she asked, already knowing the answer.

"Yes," they said in unison, which made them both laugh.

"How did you know?" Hannah asked, genuinely curious.

"Because the locals are all snug at home, holed up with their families, and only the people who didn't stock up properly are here in the store," the cashier explained as she bagged their meager groceries. "Or tourists who got caught in the storm."

Noah shook his head ruefully. "We're from Texas. We have hurricanes, not snowstorms. This one caught us completely by surprise."

The girl nodded sympathetically and then bagged their groceries with the efficiency of someone who had been doing this job for years.

"Be careful out there," she said seriously, making eye contact with both of them. "This storm is not over yet. Weather service says it's going to get worse before it gets better."

Those words settled over Noah like a bad premonition as they walked out into the parking lot, but he shook it off. They were going to be fine. They'd grab their groceries, skip the park given how cold it was, and head back to the hotel where it was warm and safe.

Once again, the snow was coming down so hard that it was difficult to find the Jeep in the now mostly empty parking lot. The world had turned into a whiteout, visibility reduced to maybe fifty feet.

When they reached the vehicle, Noah once again had to wipe the snow off the front windows and the hood, muttering under his breath about Montana weather and why anyone would voluntarily live somewhere this cold.

Just as they were about to climb into the Jeep, bags in hand and ready to escape the brutal cold, Noah heard a woman scream, high-pitched and terrified, the kind of scream that made every instinct in his body snap to attention.

Turning quickly, nearly dropping the grocery bag, he saw an elderly woman had slipped on a patch of ice hidden beneath the snow and now lay flat on her back in the parking lot, her arms and legs splayed at awkward angles.

Hannah was already running toward her, moving faster than Noah would have thought possible in snow boots, her medical training overriding everything else.

"Don't move her," Hannah yelled at the young girl who was with the fallen woman, her voice carrying the authority of someone who knew exactly what they were doing. "Don't let her sit up or move at all."

The girl, maybe twelve years old, was already down on her knees next to the woman, her face pale with fear.

"Grandma, are you all right?" the girl asked, her voice shaking, tears already streaming down her young face.

"Yes, yes, just help me up," the elderly woman said, trying to move, clearly disoriented.

Noah raced toward them, his heart pounding, his mind already running through possible injuries and treatment protocols. When he got there and dropped to his knees beside the woman, he immediately saw the pool of blood seeping from the back of her head, dark red against the white snow, spreading in a circle that was growing larger by the second. She'd taken a nasty fall, the kind of fall that could be fatal for someone her age.

"Ma'am, please don't move," Hannah said firmly but gently, placing a restraining hand on the woman's shoulder. "We're doctors and we need to make sure you're okay before you try to get up."

While Hannah talked to the woman, establishing rapport and trying to keep her calm, Noah pulled out his phone and dialed 911 with fingers that were starting to go numb from the cold.

"911, what's your emergency?"

"We have an elderly woman down in the parking lot of the Cherry Creek Grocery Store," Noah said, his voice steady and professional despite the adrenaline coursing through his system. "She's suffered a slip and fall on ice. She's got a serious head injury with blood coming from the back of her head, significant bleeding. We need an ambulance right away. This is Dr. Noah Baker, I'm a physician."

"Ambulance is on the way, doctor," the dispatcher said. "Can you tell me if she's conscious?"

"Yes, conscious and alert, but showing signs of confusion."

Hannah was already conducting her assessment, her hands moving with practiced efficiency as she talked to the woman in that calm, soothing voice she used with frightened patients.

"Until we're certain you're all right, we don't want to move you and risk making a broken bone worse or causing any spinal damage," Hannah explained. "Can you tell me what you landed on besides the back of your head?"

"My back," the woman said, wincing. "I landed hard on my back. My head is hurting so bad, it feels like it's going to split open."

"I'm certain you've suffered a concussion at minimum," Hannah said honestly. "Dr. Noah has called an ambulance. You need to be checked out properly in a hospital with imaging."

The little girl who was with her started to cry harder, her small body shaking with sobs that broke Noah's heart. This was someone's grandmother, someone's mother, lying bleeding in a grocery store parking lot.

"That's my granddaughter," the woman said, her voice weakening slightly. "Mariah, honey, call your father. Tell him what's happened. Tell him we're at the store."

Hannah had her fingers on the woman's wrist, taking her pulse, and Noah could see from the expression on her face that she didn't like what she was finding.

"I need you to take some deep breaths for me," Hannah instructed, her voice still calm but with an edge of concern that Noah recognized immediately. "Try to relax. Your heart rate is too high. I need you to calm down and breathe slowly. In through your nose, out through your mouth."

"I hurt," the woman said, her voice becoming thready. "It hurts everywhere."

"We're both doctors," Hannah told her again, maintaining eye contact, keeping her engaged. "Do you mind if I run my hands down your legs and arms to see if there are any broken bones or obvious injuries?"

"No, go ahead," the woman said. "This ice and snow are making me so cold. I can't stop shaking."

She started to tremble violently, and Noah knew immediately that wasn't good. He recognized the signs, they'd lost too much time already. Without hesitation, he took off his coat and laid it over her, tucking it around her body as best he could without moving her. He feared she was going into shock, and shock could kill someone her age just as surely as the head injury.

Where the hell was the ambulance and how long was it going to take them to get here in these conditions?

"Mariah, why don't you keep an eye out for the ambulance," Noah told the little girl gently, giving her a task to focus on so she wouldn't have to watch her grandmother deteriorate. "Stand over there by the store entrance where you can see the road, and wave to them when you see them coming, okay?"

The girl nodded, grateful to have something to do, and ran toward the building.

Noah knelt beside the woman in the cold, wet snow, feeling it soak through his jeans, and checked her pupils with his phone's flashlight. They were dilated and sluggish to respond. Definite head injury, possibly severe. Possible intracranial bleeding.

"Mrs…" he started, trying to get her to focus on him.

"Phillips," she said weakly. "Linda Phillips."

"Mrs. Phillips, how old are you?" he asked, trying to keep her talking, to keep her conscious.

"I'm seventy years old," she said, her words starting to slur slightly. "We ran out of bread, and instead of making fresh bread at home like I should have, I came to the store. How stupid is that? How stupid am I?"

"You're not stupid at all," Noah said firmly. "Mrs. Phillips, can you count backward from ten for me?"

"Ten, nine, eight," her voice stumbled, her lips trembling from cold and shock.

"Keep going," he encouraged, hoping to distract her, fearful about the amount of blood still oozing from her head wound. But he didn't dare move her without a spine board beneath her, not with a potential spinal injury.

The sound of an ambulance siren could be heard in the distance, but they were still blocks away, fighting through the same treacherous road conditions Noah had just navigated, and they needed to get here now, not in five minutes.

"Six, four, two," she said, skipping numbers, her voice trailing off into confusion.

"Mrs. Phillips, are you married?" he asked, trying a different approach to keep her engaged.

"Yes, my husband Tim told me not to go," she said, tears leaking from the corners of her eyes. "He told me to stay home, but I didn't listen. I never listen…"

She stopped talking, and Noah could see that she was getting very woozy, her eyes losing focus, her level of consciousness dropping.

"Stay with me, Mrs. Phillips," he told her urgently, leaning down into her face, making her look at him. "Take a deep breath and focus on me. Look at my eyes. Stay with me."

Hannah, who had completed her preliminary body assessment, carefully palpating arms and legs for fractures, shook her head at him, a barely perceptible movement that communicated volumes.

"I don't think you've broken your arms or legs," Hannah told Mrs. Phillips, "but your back, I'm still concerned about your spine, so we're absolutely not going to move you until the paramedics get here with proper equipment."

"Heart rate is way too high," she mouthed silently to Noah. "Shock."

The woman was definitely going into shock, her body's response to trauma overwhelming her system. And then, as if to confirm Noah's worst fears, her body began to shake violently, convulsing.

"I can't breathe," Mrs. Phillips gasped, her hands clutching at her chest. "Something's wrong. I can't—"

Noah put his hand on her chest, feeling for the heartbeat, and his own heart sank. "I think she's going into cardiac arrest."

The ambulance pulled up at that exact moment, lights flashing, and Noah had never been so grateful to see emergency responders in his life.

"Bring a defibrillator," Hannah yelled, her voice carrying across the parking lot. "We need it now. And a long spine board. She's in cardiac arrest."

The woman's eyes closed and Noah feared they were going to lose her right here in this parking lot, that this grandmother who'd just wanted to buy bread for her family was going to die in the snow.

The paramedics came running with their tactical medical kit, moving with practiced efficiency despite the conditions. One man carried a defibrillator, already turning it on.

"Dr. Noah Baker and Dr. Hannah Young," Noah told them,

standing and getting out of the way so they could work, but staying close in case they needed help. "The patient is Linda Phillips; she's seventy years old. The patient fell here in the parking lot on ice approximately five minutes ago and smacked the back of her head on the pavement, significant bleeding from the scalp laceration. We've not moved her for fear of a spinal injury. Her heart rate was elevated, respirations shallow, signs of shock, and she just went into what appears to be full cardiac arrest within the last thirty seconds."

The paramedics looked at them with expressions of both surprise and gratitude, surprised to find doctors on scene, grateful for the detailed report and the fact that Mrs. Phillips hadn't been moved.

The head paramedic took out his stethoscope and listened to her chest for a few seconds that felt like an eternity.

"Get the paddles out now," he called to his partner. "She's in full arrest. No pulse, no respirations."

"Stand back," he yelled to everyone around them, opening Mrs. Phillips's coat and ripping her blouse open to expose her chest. Once he had the paddles positioned correctly, he yelled, "Clear!"

Everyone stepped back, and the woman's body jumped as the electricity coursed through her, her back arching off the ground in a way that made Noah cringe, fearful they had just caused damage to her spinal cord if it was indeed broken. But at least they were trying to keep her alive.

The paramedic put his stethoscope back on her chest, listening intently.

"She's back," he announced, and Noah felt relief wash over him. "Sinus rhythm. Let's get her to Missoula General now. We need to move fast."

They worked together to slide the backboard beneath her with minimal movement, strapped her head down with blocks and tape to immobilize her cervical spine, secured her body to the board, and then lifted her onto the waiting stretcher with practiced efficiency.

"This is her granddaughter," Hannah told them, pointing to Mariah, who had come running back when she saw the ambulance arrive. "Did you call your father, honey?"

"Yes," Mariah said, staring at her grandmother in disbelief, her young face pale and streaked with tears. "He's on his way to the hospital."

"She can ride in the front of the ambulance," the lead paramedic said, his voice kind despite the urgency of the situation.

Hannah nodded, putting a hand on the girl's shoulder.

"Your grandmother is in good hands," Hannah told Mariah. "You were very brave today. She's going to get the help she needs now."

"Good luck," Noah added, trying to give the girl some hope to hold onto.

The paramedics loaded Mrs. Phillips into the back of the ambulance, and Mariah climbed into the front seat. Within seconds, they were pulling away, lights flashing and siren wailing, racing toward the hospital through the snowstorm.

Noah, who was now shivering violently, grabbed his coat from where the paramedics had removed it. The coat was soaked with melted snow and spotted with blood, but it was better than nothing.

"I'm going to need this," he said, his teeth chattering as he put it back on. "Even if it is soaking wet."

Standing in the parking lot, Noah and Hannah watched until the ambulance disappeared into the curtain of falling snow, and then they slowly walked back to the Jeep, both of them processing what had just happened.

"Even in Montana, we can't seem to get away from being a doctor," Hannah said quietly, and Noah heard the exhaustion in her voice that mirrored his own.

"Nope," Noah replied, opening the passenger door for her

before walking around to the driver's side. "And I'm frozen to my core. I think I want to skip the outside snow activities."

"Agreed," Hannah said, climbing into the Jeep gratefully. "It's kind of lost its excitement after that. I've always heard that falls in the elderly could be very dangerous, but that's the first time I've actually experienced one that severe outside of a hospital setting."

Glancing at him as he started the engine and cranked the heat up as high as it would go, she shook her head.

"Take me back to the hotel. I want to watch a happy movie and pretend the outside world doesn't exist for a while."

As they climbed into the Jeep and Noah carefully backed out of the parking space, he glanced over at Hannah. They worked together very well. They always had, from the very beginning of their relationship as colleagues. Even after becoming a couple, or whatever they were now, there was nothing to argue about when they were working on a patient. They operated in perfect sync, anticipating each other's moves, trusting each other's judgment completely.

Could they work full-time together like that and not argue the way his parents had? His mother and father had been partners in their practice, and it had destroyed their marriage slowly, painfully, over years of competing and criticizing and trying to prove who was the better physician. Every patient had become a point of contention. Every diagnosis a source of argument. Every treatment plan a battle of wills.

But watching Hannah today, seeing how seamlessly they'd worked together to help Mrs. Phillips, Noah wondered if maybe it didn't have to be that way. Maybe his parents' marriage had failed not because they worked together, but because they'd never learned how to be partners instead of competitors.

Maybe, with the right person, it could actually work.

The thought both terrified and thrilled him as he drove them carefully back through the snow toward the hotel, toward warmth and safety and whatever came next.

CHAPTER 9

*H*annah loved being a doctor. It had been her lifelong dream, cultivated since she was eight years old and watched a surgeon save her brother's life after a terrible car accident. But there were days, days like today, when she had to deal with life-and-death situations that reminded her just how fragile human existence really was, how quickly everything could change in the span of a single heartbeat.

The poor woman had no idea how close she'd come to dying today. All from a simple slip on the ice. Something so ordinary, so mundane, going to the grocery store for bread, had nearly ended her life. Her head had hit the concrete hard, and her heart had not taken the stress of the cold and the fall well at all. If she and Noah had not been there, if they'd decided to stay in the hotel room for just five more minutes, if they'd chosen a different store, Mrs. Phillips might have died alone in that parking lot with only her terrified granddaughter watching helplessly.

The thought made Hannah's stomach clench with a mixture of grief and gratitude.

Lying on that cold concrete in the snow with a concussion and a possible underlying heart condition had been too much for the elderly woman's body, and she'd gone into cardiac arrest right there in front of them. Hannah had seen it happen, the exact moment when Mrs. Phillips's eyes had gone unfocused, when her breathing had stopped, when death had reached out to claim her.

But they'd fought back. She and Noah had fought back, and they'd won. At least for now.

As they walked back into their hotel room, they were both silent, wrapped in their own thoughts. Hannah could see that their outing had affected both of them deeply, that the weight of what they'd just experienced was settling over them like the snow settling over Montana. They'd decided against going to the park and building a snowman, and she was glad. The idea of playing in the snow, of being carefree and laughing, felt wrong now. Fighting to save that woman's life had drained her both emotionally and physically, leaving her feeling hollowed out and raw.

After she closed the door behind them, shutting out the cold and the world, Hannah sank down on the bed without even removing her coat. Her legs simply wouldn't hold her anymore. Even now, she knew the ER doctors were busy doing their best to save Mrs. Phillips's life, running tests, performing scans, and trying to determine the extent of her injuries. Even now her family was rushing through the snowstorm to reach her and be by her side, probably terrified, probably praying. And her granddaughter, sweet little Mariah, was alone in the waiting room, anxious for family to arrive, replaying the horror of watching her grandmother collapse over and over in her young mind.

Maybe Hannah should have gone to the hospital with the little girl. The thought had been nagging at her since the ambulance drove away, a persistent whisper of guilt that she couldn't quite silence. But the child didn't really know Hannah. All she knew was that Hannah and Noah had helped her grandmother, that they were doctors who had appeared when needed. They were complete strangers, really. Would her presence have been a comfort or just another source of confusion for the traumatized girl?

Noah sank down on the bed beside her, and she felt the mattress dip with his weight. They both reclined against the headrest, staring up at the ceiling, neither one quite ready to look at the other yet.

"We did the best we could," Noah said finally, his voice rough with emotion he was trying to hide.

"Yes," Hannah said softly, though the word felt inadequate. "Maybe I should have ridden with the little girl to the hospital. She looked so scared, Noah. So alone."

"They didn't have room for you and her in the ambulance," he pointed out gently, "and she couldn't ride in the Jeep with us because she didn't know us. Her father wouldn't have wanted his daughter getting into a vehicle with strangers, no matter how well-intentioned."

"True," Hannah replied, knowing he was right but still feeling the sting of regret. "I just hate to see kids in situations like this where they're alone until family arrives. I keep thinking about her sitting in that waiting room, not knowing if her grandmother is going to live or die, wondering if she should have done something differently."

They lay side by side on the bed together, close but not quite touching. Hannah could feel the warmth radiating from his body, could hear his breathing gradually slowing as the adrenaline began to fade from his system. He reached out and took her hand, lacing his fingers through hers, and she held on tight, needing that connection more than she'd realized.

"If we hadn't been there, she wouldn't have had a chance," Noah said quietly, squeezing her hand. "You know that, right? Without immediate intervention, without you keeping her calm and me calling for help, without both of us recognizing she was going into shock, she would have died in that parking lot."

"You're right," Hannah acknowledged, feeling some of the

guilt begin to lift. "She was trying to get up when I reached her side. She didn't realize how bad she was, didn't understand that moving could have made everything worse. But there was so much blood gathering beneath her head, pooling in the snow."

"Yes, I saw that," Noah said, his voice tight with the memory. "I'm sorry we didn't go play in the snow afterward. I know you really wanted to build that snowman."

Hannah turned her head to look at him, studying his profile in the grey afternoon light filtering through the window. That was the least of her concerns right now. After watching that elderly woman lying there, struggling for every breath, fighting for her life, Hannah had been reminded with brutal clarity that in an instant, everything could change. Life could be stolen away without warning, without mercy, without time to say the things that needed to be said.

It made her even more certain that she wanted something real with Noah. Something solid and lasting. She wanted to stop pretending this was casual, stop acting like they were just colleagues with benefits, just friends who fell into bed together. There was something growing between them, something that deserved to be acknowledged and nurtured and given room to flourish. She wanted them to be a couple, not just in private, not just for weekends stolen away from reality, but a real couple who everyone knew about. A couple who she hoped would eventually marry, have a family, spend holidays together, grow old together, and build a life that mattered.

It was past time to make a commitment to one another or for her to move on and stop letting herself hope for something Noah might not be capable of giving.

The thought terrified her, but she knew it was true. She couldn't keep doing this indefinitely, couldn't keep falling deeper in love with him while pretending she didn't care whether he loved her back.

"After helping her, I wasn't in the mood for playing," Hannah said honestly. "And you had been without a coat for way longer than you should've been, Noah. You gave her your coat without even thinking about it. Are you warm now?"

She could feel him shivering slightly beside her, his body still trying to recover from the prolonged exposure to the brutal cold. Without waiting for an answer, Hannah moved closer, letting him pull her across the bed and wrap his arms around her, spooning her against his chest. She could feel his heart beating against her back, steady and strong, and it reassured her in a way nothing else could.

Rising slightly, she pulled the thick comforter on the bed over both of them, cocooning them in warmth and softness. She could feel him shaking, small tremors running through his body.

"Now I am," he said, his breath warm against her neck, and she felt him gradually begin to relax as his body temperature started to normalize.

The curtains were still open, and Hannah could see the snow continuing to fall outside their window, blanketing the world in white, muffling all sound, creating the illusion that they were the only two people left in the universe.

"I'm glad we went to the store," Hannah said softly, meaning it with every fiber of her being. "I'm glad we were there for that woman. I'm glad we were in the right place at exactly the right time."

"Yes," Noah agreed, his arms tightening around her. "We probably saved a life today. Actually, I'd say we definitely saved a life today."

"Those are the good days," Hannah said, feeling emotion well up in her throat. "The days when you know you've made a real difference, when you've helped someone in a way that matters. Those are the days that remind you why you went into medicine in the first place."

There were also days, too many days, when you felt like the heavens had opened and were pulling everyone you tried to save away from Earth, no matter how hard you fought to hold on to them. Days where no matter what you did, no matter how skilled you were or how hard you tried or how much you wanted it, your patient died anyway. Those days, Hannah hated with a passion that still surprised her. Those were the days that made her question everything, that made her wonder if she was strong enough to keep doing this job year after year.

With a shiver that had nothing to do with the cold, Hannah tried to erase what had happened today from her mind, not the memory of helping Mrs. Phillips, which she would treasure, but the visceral fear she'd felt watching the woman code, the helplessness that had threatened to overwhelm her, the reminder of mortality that had shaken her more than she wanted to admit.

Time to think of something more pleasant. Something that would tell her more about the man holding her, the man she was falling in love with despite all her efforts to protect her heart. She wanted to know him better, wanted to understand what had shaped him into the person he was today.

"Tell me your favorite Christmas memory," Hannah said, deliberately changing the subject to get their minds off the elderly woman and the uncertainty of whether she would survive the night.

There was a long moment of silence, and Hannah wondered if Noah was going to answer at all. She could feel the tension in his body, could sense him reaching back into his past, sifting through memories both good and bad.

"I was maybe seven years old," he finally said, his voice softer now, almost wistful, "and I'd asked Santa to bring me a bicycle. All the kids in the neighborhood had one but me, and I felt so left out. They'd ride around together after school and on weekends, having adventures, going places, and I'd just watch from the porch. My mother told me in no uncertain terms that she treated too many children who had broken bones from bicycles, that she'd seen too many head injuries and shattered limbs. She was absolutely not going to buy me one, no matter how much I begged. So I asked Santa instead, hoping maybe he'd overrule her."

Hannah's heart ached for that little boy, desperate for something so simple, something every other child seemed to have. "What kind of doctor was your mother?" she asked, wanting to understand the woman who had shaped Noah's childhood.

"A pediatrician," Noah said, and Hannah could hear the complexity of emotions in those two words, love, frustration, grief, anger, all tangled together. "And so was my father, though he did more general medicine. He was more of a family doctor, really. They had a practice together."

Now Hannah remembered. They'd had a medical practice together until the divorce, working side by side every day, their professional and personal lives completely intertwined. Noah had mentioned it one time, briefly, but he never talked much about his family. She knew the basics, the divorce when he was a teenager, the years of conflict, the way medicine had both united and divided his parents. And then, years later, the tragedy. Suddenly, Hannah recalled with painful clarity that his mother had committed suicide, and Noah had been devastated to think he hadn't seen the signs of her distress, hadn't recognized that she was in crisis, hadn't been able to save her the way he saved strangers in the ER every day.

But Hannah wasn't going to mention that now. Not when they were both already emotionally raw from the day's events.

"So did Santa deliver?" she asked instead, keeping her voice light.

Noah laughed, a genuine sound that made her smile. "One day, my father and I were talking, it must have been Christmas Eve, though I didn't realize it at the time, and he wanted to know what I'd asked for from Santa. I remember that conversation like it was yesterday, and I can still picture exactly where we were sitting, what he was wearing. I told him that all the other kids in the neighborhood had bikes, and Mother told me I couldn't have one because it was too dangerous. So I asked Santa to bring me one, thinking surely Santa would understand how important it was."

Hannah felt him tense against her, his body going rigid with the memory, and she waited, giving him space to continue.

"Years later, after my mother died, he told me the rest of the story," Noah continued, his voice thick with emotion. "That was Christmas Eve when I told him about the bike. Somehow, he slipped out that very night and went to every store still open, finally finding a bike at the last possible minute before they closed. After my mother went to bed, exhausted from her shift at the hospital, he stayed up until three in the morning putting it together in the garage, trying to be quiet, trying not to wake anyone. The next morning, I was so incredibly excited, jumping around the living room like a maniac. Santa had delivered! Santa had brought me a bike! I thought I was the luckiest kid in the world."

He paused, and Hannah could hear the pain in the silence.

"Later that night, after the excitement wore off, I heard my parents fighting in their bedroom. I was in my room playing with my new bike, I'd actually brought it inside because I didn't want to let it out of my sight, and I could hear them yelling at each other through the walls. But I didn't know what they were fighting about, didn't understand the words. I just knew they were angry. It wasn't until years later that my father told me the truth. That fight was about the bike. My father had gone against my mother's explicit wishes and purchased me a bike without her knowledge or permission. She felt betrayed, undermined, like he'd chosen me over her. He felt like she was being unreasonable, overprotective, like she couldn't see past the worst-case scenarios to let me just be a kid."

While Hannah could understand his mother wanting to keep her child safe, what parent didn't want that? All kids loved bikes.

It was a rite of passage, a symbol of freedom and independence. And yes, Hannah had treated her fair share of broken bones in the ER from kids who'd fallen off their bikes, had seen the road rash and the concussions and the occasional more serious injury. But that was part of life, part of growing up. Kids took chances, experimented with their limits, and sometimes they paid the price. But you couldn't protect them from everything, couldn't wrap them in bubble wrap and expect them to grow into functional adults.

"Did you ever get hurt riding your bike?" Hannah asked softly, already suspecting she knew the answer.

"Yes," Noah admitted, "but I never told my mother. I fell off during the first week I had it, took a corner too fast, trying to keep up with the older kids, and skinned my knees up really badly. Blood everywhere, gravel embedded in the skin, the works. I was terrified she'd take the bike away if she found out. So I told my father, and he doctored me up in the bathroom while she was at work, cleaned out the wounds, bandaged me up, swore me to secrecy. We kept it our secret. We often kept secrets from my mother, actually. Little things, like when I didn't finish my vegetables or when I stayed up past my bedtime reading under the covers with a flashlight. She loved me fiercely, I never doubted that for a second, but she knew too many dangers, had seen too many terrible things in her practice. She tried to protect me from a world that she saw as fundamentally unsafe, and in doing so, she sometimes protected me from living."

Noah had stopped shivering now, his body finally warm again. Hannah rolled over carefully, untangling herself from his embrace so she could face him, so she could gaze into those blue eyes that had her own heart skipping a beat every time she looked into them. They were beautiful eyes, expressive and intelligent, but they also held shadows —the weight of loss, disappointment, and deferred dreams.

"You and your father are close," Hannah said. It wasn't a question.

"Yes," Noah confirmed, a small smile touching his lips. "And I'm genuinely happy that he's found someone who makes him happy, someone who brings joy into his life. Though he and my mother divorced years ago, I always thought he still loved her in some way, carried a torch for the woman she'd been before the bitterness and the fighting consumed everything good between them. I think he even tried to take care of her after the divorce, checking in on her, making sure she was okay. He felt responsible for her somehow, even after she'd pushed him away. But life was undeniably better after he and mother split. There wasn't as much screaming and yelling in the house, wasn't the constant tension of waiting for the next fight to erupt. The silence was actually peaceful instead of ominous."

Hannah couldn't imagine living with a parent who screamed and yelled regularly, who filled the house with anger and conflict. Her own parents had their disagreements, certainly, but they'd always handled them quietly, rationally, with respect for each other and awareness that their children were listening. She'd never met Noah's mother, had never had the chance, but she'd never forget the night the woman killed herself. An overdose of pills, carefully planned and executed. No cry for help, no last-minute change of heart. No one had found her until it was too late, until there was nothing anyone could do.

But maybe now she was at peace. Maybe now, wherever she was, the demons that had haunted her were finally silent.

Noah's mouth descended on Hannah's, cutting off her melancholy thoughts, and she welcomed the distraction, welcomed the heat that immediately sparked between them. He rolled over on top of her, his weight pressing her into the mattress, solid and real and alive. Their mouths came apart for a moment, both of them breathing hard, and he took her wrists gently into his hands and raised her arms above her head, pinning them there, not forcefully, but with clear intent. The gesture was both dominant and vulnerable, asking permission while taking control.

"Is there something you want, Dr. Noah?" Hannah asked breathlessly, her body already responding to his proximity, to the desire she could see burning in his eyes.

"You," he said simply, his voice rough with need. "I want to be inside you. I want to forget about everything else for a while and just feel you, just be with you."

A smile came over Hannah's face, slow and seductive. She could feel the hardness of him pressed against her thigh, could see the hunger in his expression, and it made her feel powerful and desired and cherished all at once.

"Then you're going to have to work for it," she teased, her voice dropping to a sultry whisper. "Show me how much you want me, Noah. Prove it."

He chuckled, the sound low and promising, sending shivers of anticipation down her spine.

"My pleasure," Noah said, and then his mouth was on hers again, and Hannah stopped thinking entirely, lost herself in sensation, in the feeling of being wanted and needed and maybe, just maybe, loved.

Outside, the snow continued to fall, but inside their small sanctuary, they created their own warmth, their own shelter from the storm. And for now, for this moment, it was enough.

CHAPTER 10

She lifted her mouth to his, and he met her halfway. It was a kiss of desperation and longing, and it took Noah completely by surprise with its intensity, its urgency, its raw need. Her mouth covered his, moving over his lips with a hunger that went beyond simple desire, seeking comfort he was more than willing to give, craving connection in the wake of what they'd just witnessed. While they dealt with death on an everyday basis, it was woven into the very fabric of their profession, sometimes you were still shocked at how quickly it could come, how easily a life could slip away, how fragile the thread was that kept each person tethered to this world.

Noah was eager to soothe her and remind her she was still alive, that they were both still here, still breathing, still capable of feeling and touching and loving. What they had done today was a good deed, a moment of grace in a chaotic universe. Once again, they'd beaten death back, pushed it away from someone who deserved more time, and that felt good. It felt powerful and meaningful and right.

Lying on top of her, Noah could feel the soft crush of Hannah's breasts against his chest, could feel every curve of her body pressed against his, and the sweet scent of vanilla enveloped him like a familiar embrace. It was her signature scent, the one that lingered in his car after she'd been a passenger, the one that clung to his clothes after they'd been together. Holding her hands in his, her arms raised above her head in a gesture of trust and surrender, his mouth ravaged hers, demanding she give herself over to the moment, wanting her to feel the passion flowing through him like electricity, wanting her to know without words how much she meant to him.

Releasing her hands, Noah pushed her sweater up, needing to feel her breasts in his hands, needing skin-to-skin contact, needing to touch her in ways that affirmed life and connection and the beautiful simplicity of two bodies coming together.

Hannah moaned, the sound encouraging him, spurring him on as her hands reached beneath his shirt and she let her fingernails gently rake across his skin, leaving trails of fire in their wake. The sensation sent shivers down his spine, made his nerve endings sing with pleasure.

Their lips broke apart for a moment, and Noah rose up enough to yank his sweater over his head, tossing it carelessly to the floor. Hannah leaned up, and he removed her sweater as well, his hands trembling slightly with anticipation, leaving her in just her bra.

The woman wore the sexiest underwear he'd ever seen, and he'd been enjoying taking them off since yesterday, revealing her inch by beautiful inch, discovering her body like a treasure map he wanted to memorize.

Noah leaned over and kissed the tops of her breasts that spilled forth from her bra cups, soft and warm and perfect. His tongue trailed over her smooth skin, tasting salt and sweetness, and she leaned back, giving him access to her throat, offering herself to him. Eagerly, he took her cue and kissed his way across her chest and up the column of her neck, lingering at her ear where he knew she was especially sensitive.

He wanted to make her feel good, wanted to erase the images of Mrs. Phillips lying in the snow from both their minds. He wanted to comfort Hannah and make the demons from the day disappear into nothing. He wanted to remove all dark thoughts and envelop her in pure sensual pleasure, wanted to give her a reason to smile, to laugh, to remember that life was also beautiful and worth living. And he needed the same thing, needed to lose himself in her, needed to forget everything but the feeling of her skin against his, her breath mingling with his, her heartbeat synchronized with his own.

All he desired was to experience being in her arms once again. Just once more, he told himself, even though he knew it was a lie. Once more, and then he could step away, he promised himself, even though he had no intention of stepping away. But did he want to stop being with her? Could he even if he tried?

This woman was his best friend, his confidant, the person he trusted most in the world, and now she was his lover. And the thought of being without her, of going back to the way things were before this weekend, left a gaping void in his heart that terrified him. Oh, how he'd like to make her his permanently, to build a life with her, to wake up beside her every morning for the rest of his life. But he feared becoming like his parents, feared the screaming matches and the resentment and the slow death of love that he'd witnessed growing up. He knew with absolute certainty that he would never accept a marriage where they screamed at one another, where work became more important than the relationship, where competition replaced partnership.

But was he strong enough to risk it? Strong enough to believe that he and Hannah could be different?

She disentangled her limbs from his and stood beside the bed, and Noah watched her, transfixed. Slowly, deliberately, maintaining eye contact in a way that made his breath catch, she slid down the zipper on her jeans and stepped out of them with graceful movements, leaving them pooled on the floor. She stood before him, beautiful and confident in her matching panties and bra, and Noah felt his heart skip a beat.

"God, Hannah, you're stunning," he said hoarsely, reaching for her, needing her back in bed with him, needing to feel her weight against him again. "You're absolutely breathtaking."

She took his hand and pulled him until he was standing, their bodies close but not quite touching, the air between them crackling with tension and anticipation. Then she unbuttoned his jeans with steady fingers and slid them down his legs along with his boxers, her hands brushing against his skin as she worked, driving him crazy with every touch.

"God," she whispered, her voice thick with desire as she pressed against him, skin to skin at last. "I want you so badly, Noah. I need you."

Urgently, his hands pushed her bra down, freeing her breasts for his taking, and he cupped them reverently before his mouth wrapped around her nipple. He suckled until she moaned, the sound going straight to his groin, and he felt himself harden even more, felt the desperate need to be inside her building to an almost unbearable level.

Her hands tugged him tightly against her, her fingers digging into his back, and he was forced to release her breast, forced to come up for air.

"I want you now," Noah told her, his voice rough and urgent as he reached for the nightstand, fumbling for the box of condoms they'd opened yesterday. "I need to be inside you. I need to feel you around me."

Her green eyes had darkened to the color of a forest at twilight, and her breathing was quick and heavy, her chest rising and falling rapidly. They had barely touched one another compared to their first time together, but she was already ready, already wanting him as much as he wanted her.

Falling back onto the bed together, they crawled beneath the covers, seeking warmth and privacy even though they were alone, creating their own little world. The moment she touched him intimately, Noah knew he would be on fire. A sexual blaze that would cloud his rational thinking and take over his body completely, making him forget everything but the need to be joined with her. A heat he would welcome, a fire he wanted to burn in.

He lay beside her, his mouth hungrily seeking hers while he ran his hands over her body, memorizing every curve, every dip, every place that made her gasp or sigh. She wrapped her fingers around his shaft, and Noah moaned as she stroked him, the pleasure so intense it was almost painful. He didn't want her to stop, God, he never wanted her to stop, but he had to put the condom on before he lost all control.

Quickly, his hands shaking slightly, he tore open the package and sheathed himself, hating even the brief separation.

His fingers found her womanly center and caressed her gently at first, then with increasing pressure and speed as she gasped and writhed upon the bed, her hips rising to meet his touch, silently begging for more.

"Oh," she cried out, her voice breaking. "Noah, please."

His lips tasted her skin everywhere he could reach, her shoulder, her collarbone, the sensitive spot behind her ear. He drank in her beauty with his eyes while his fingers danced over her clit with practiced movements, learning what she liked, what made her breath catch, what made her call out his name. Soon her body tensed, every muscle going rigid, and then she shuddered beneath his fingers as waves of pleasure washed over her.

"Noah," she cried, reaching her release, and he smiled with satisfaction, with the knowledge that he'd given her this, that he'd brought her to this peak of pleasure.

"Did I work hard enough for it?" he asked, his voice a velvety whisper against her flushed skin, teasing her with her own earlier words.

A deep-throated laugh came from her, rich and satisfied. "You did perfect. You always do perfect."

He grinned and kissed her on the lips, soft and sweet this time, before he released her and started to move over her.

"I want to be on top," Hannah said suddenly, her hand on his chest, stopping him. She rolled him over onto his back with surprising strength.

She rose to her knees and straddled Noah, positioning herself above him, and he looked up at her in awe. The sight of her like this, powerful and beautiful and completely in control, was almost enough to undo him right there.

Right now, Noah would do anything she asked of him. He would give her the moon if she wanted it, would rearrange the stars to spell out her name. Today, together they had worked to save a woman's life, had fought death and won, and he needed Hannah to help him put the scene from that parking lot out of his head, needed her to anchor him to this moment, to life, to hope. Right now, every emotion, every feeling, every thought centered on Hannah. This woman, who had gone from being a friend to being a lover so seamlessly that he couldn't remember exactly when the transition had happened. This woman who held his heart in her hands without even realizing it, and he feared what would happen next, feared what it would mean when this weekend ended and they had to return to reality.

They had so much to work out, logistics, and expectations and definitions of what they were to each other. And yet all he wanted, all he needed, was to be in her arms, to feel her body against his, to hear her say his name in that breathy way she did when she was close to climax.

The thought of coming home to Hannah after a long, exhausting day at the hospital seemed like heaven, seemed like the kind of future he'd given up dreaming about years ago. The idea of sharing meals with her, of falling asleep beside her every night, of building something real and lasting together, it was everything he'd ever wanted but been too afraid to reach for.

And yet his parents had once felt the same way, hadn't they? They'd been in love once, young and hopeful and confident they could handle anything together. Would the job destroy his relationship with Hannah the same way it had destroyed his parents' marriage? Would they end up competing instead of collaborating? Would their love turn to resentment when the pressures of their career became too much?

Hannah slid over him slowly, taking him inside her inch by inch, and his penis fit snugly inside her warmth. The rush of pleasure, intense and overwhelming, almost sent him over the edge immediately. With every stroke, every movement of her hips, his heart filled more and more with an emotion he was terrified to name as he spiraled closer and closer to the edge of control.

He wanted to take her to new heights of pleasure, wanted to give her everything she'd ever wanted, everything she deserved. He wanted to give her his all, his body, his heart, his future, his soul. And so he did as she rode him, his hands on her breasts, his heart in his eyes for anyone to see, all his defenses stripped away. His soul was branded with her name, marked forever. Together forever, he thought, and the words didn't frighten him the way they should have.

"Hannah," Noah said out loud, needing to hear her name on his lips, and he gazed into her desire-filled eyes, holding her gaze as the two of them rode the crest of desire together, climbing higher and higher toward something that felt like more than just physical pleasure.

Her muscles clenched around him, gripping him tightly, and he knew she was coming. He was determined to go with her, to share this moment completely. Staring into her eyes, refusing to look away, Noah exploded inside her with an intensity that shook him to his core, and then her own climax ripped through her as she called out his name like a prayer, like a benediction, like a promise.

With a mighty slam, he ground into her one last time, giving her everything he had, and then she collapsed on top of him, her body slumping, her breathing heavy and labored as he wrapped his arms around her and held her close, held her like he never wanted to let go.

Would it be like this forever? If so, how could he ever walk away? How could he ever go back to a life without this, without her? They were one, connected in ways that went far beyond the physical, bound together by something he didn't fully understand but couldn't deny.

For several minutes, they didn't move, didn't speak, just lay there feeling each other breathe, feeling their hearts beat in tandem. Then Noah pulled out of her gently and rolled her to her side, spooning her the way they'd been lying earlier, creating a cocoon of warmth and safety. They lay together, catching their breaths, their hearts slowly returning to earth from whatever stratosphere they'd reached together.

"Hannah," Noah said softly, whispering her name against her ear, needing to break the silence before it became too heavy with unspoken words. "Where do we go from here?"

It was the question that had been haunting him since yesterday, since they'd first crossed this line together. What did this mean? What were they now? Could they go back to being just friends, or had they destroyed that foundation by adding this new dimension to their relationship?

She smiled, and he could hear it in her voice even though he couldn't see her face. "To Whitefish to spend Christmas with your father and new stepmother."

That wasn't the answer he was searching for, and Noah felt a pang of disappointment mixed with relief. Then again, he didn't know exactly what he wanted her to say. He didn't know what answer would satisfy the questions swirling in his mind. Their relationship had changed so rapidly, from colleagues to friends to this, whatever this was, and he was so damn afraid. Afraid of losing her, afraid of keeping her, afraid of repeating his parents' mistakes, afraid of missing his one chance at real happiness.

She knew some of what had happened between his parents, the fighting, the divorce, the way medicine had poisoned their love. But she didn't know the full story, didn't know the darkest parts, the secrets that haunted him late at night. And that was what frightened him most of all.

Would she continue to want to be with him when he told her the truth? Would she still look at him the same way when she knew everything, all the ugly, painful details he'd kept hidden for so long? Or would she realize that he was damaged, broken in ways that couldn't be fixed, destined to repeat the cycles of dysfunction he'd grown up watching?

Noah tightened his arms around her, holding her close, trying to memorize the feeling of her in his arms. Because he knew that he would have to tell her everything eventually, soon. And when he did, there was a very real chance that this, whatever this beautiful, fragile thing between them was, would shatter into a thousand irreparable pieces.

But for now, for this moment, he had her. And he was going to hold on to her for as long as she'd let him.

CHAPTER 11

The next day, Noah took her to the park, and Hannah felt like a weight had been lifted from her shoulders. The snow was starting to taper off, the storm finally beginning to lose its fury. There were fewer deluges, fewer moments when the wind whipped the flakes into blinding curtains of white. Though the white flakes continued to come down, drifting lazily from the grey sky, it wasn't as heavy as it had been. The world felt softer somehow, quieter, like everything was holding its breath.

Jumping out of the jeep the moment Noah put it in park, Hannah ran into the park with the enthusiasm of a child on Christmas morning. She started to make snowballs immediately, her hands already going numb inside her gloves, but not caring one bit. She rolled one along the ground, pushing it ahead of her, watching as it grew bigger and bigger with each rotation, gathering more snow, becoming more substantial. Each one grew bigger until she had a huge lump of packed snow, perfectly round and ready to become the base of her snowman.

"Come on," she cried out, laughing so hard her sides hurt. "Come help me, Noah!"

He stood off to the side with his phone held up, recording her, and she could see the amused smile on his face even from this distance.

"And this is Dr. Hannah Young, respected emergency room physician, acting like she's ten years old, making a snowman," he narrated in his best documentary voice.

The man was way too serious most of the time, Hannah thought with affection. Always thinking, always analyzing, always holding something back. And yet, he was so damn smart, so competent, so good at everything he did that she feared getting hurt by him. Not physically, never that. But rather emotionally. Because right now, after these last few days together, all he'd done was confirm what she'd been trying to deny for months: she was absolutely, completely, irrevocably in love with him.

But if he chose to walk away when this weekend ended, if he decided that what they had was just a temporary escape from reality, she'd be devastated. Shattered. She wasn't sure she'd recover.

Finally, deciding to take matters into her own hands, Hannah picked up a handful of snow and formed a ball in her gloved hands, packing it tight. She wound up like a pitcher and threw it at him with all her might.

It hit him square in the shoulder, and he looked at her with mock outrage.

"Hey, that's war," he cried, lowering his phone and grinning at her.

"Then get over here and help me," Hannah laughed, her joy bubbling over. "Or does the big bad Texas boy have no idea how to make a snowman?"

She figured that was probably part of the problem. Houston didn't see snow, ever. Mainly ice, and even that was only every five to ten years, and people acted like the world was ending when it happened. He'd probably never made a snowman in his entire life, had probably never experienced the simple pleasure of playing in the snow like this.

Finally, he was by her side, brushing snow off his shoulder and trying to look stern but failing completely. His eyes were sparkling with laughter.

"Okay, snow expert," he said. "What do I do?"

"We have to lift this packed ball of snow and set it on top of the other one," Hannah explained, gesturing to the large base she'd created and the slightly smaller second ball she'd been working on.

Together, they bent down and lifted the ball, their gloved hands touching as they worked, and Hannah felt that familiar spark of electricity between them. They placed the ball carefully on the first big fat ball, and quickly, she patted snow around the seam to make it stick together, her movements practiced from childhood memories.

The last time she'd made a snowman, Hannah realized with a start, she'd been in high school. Her senior year, during that freak snowstorm that had blanketed her hometown in Oklahoma. Too many years ago. Where had the time gone?

Other people were out in the park too, families with sleds, children throwing snowballs, couples walking hand in hand, all enjoying a break from being cooped up inside. This was their third day of being trapped indoors by the storm, and everyone seemed grateful for the reprieve. This morning, Hannah had awoken with Noah's arm draped over her waist and wondered, hoped, dreamed, that if they were to marry, would their lives always be this happy? Would every morning feel like this, warm and safe and full of possibility? That's what she wanted more than anything. This. Forever.

"What now?" Noah asked, interrupting her thoughts, looking at their partially constructed snowman with the concentration of a surgeon studying an X-ray.

"Now we make a smaller ball of snow to put on top for the head," she said, already starting to roll another ball.

Already her hands and feet were getting cold despite her winter gear, the chill seeping through layers of fabric. They wouldn't be able to stay out much longer, frostbite was a real danger at these temperatures, and as a doctor, she knew better than to risk it. But for now, for just a little while longer, she wanted to live in this moment, wanted to be carefree and silly and not worry about anything beyond building the perfect snowman.

When Noah lifted the smaller ball and carefully placed it on top, creating a slightly lopsided but charming head, Hannah went searching for twigs to use for arms and even the nose. She found some perfect branches under a nearby tree, their bark dark against the white snow, and carried them back triumphantly.

In a few moments, they had him all put together, a slightly wonky but undeniably endearing snowman. For the mouth, Hannah took out the lipstick she'd tucked into her coat pocket and drew a wide smile on his snowy face. It didn't look too bad, actually. Kind of quirky and charming.

"Are you done?" Noah asked, surveying their creation with what looked like genuine pride.

"With the snowman," Hannah said, grinning at him. "Let's take pictures. No one back in Texas will believe we actually did this."

Taking out his phone, they huddled close together and took several selfies, serious ones, silly ones, ones where they kissed with the snowman photobombing in the background. Hannah wondered if their friends would realize what had happened between them when they saw these pictures. Would the change be visible? Would people see the way she looked at him now and know that everything had shifted?

"Now we need to make snow angels," Hannah announced suddenly, seized by inspiration.

"What?" Noah looked at her like she'd suggested they strip naked and run through the park.

Without answering, Hannah dropped backward into the snow

and moved her arms and legs in sweeping motions, creating the wings and the gown of an angel. The cold snow against her back made her gasp, but she kept moving, kept laughing.

"You're crazy," Noah said, but she could hear the affection in his voice. "You're going to freeze to death."

Laughter bubbled from Hannah, pure and unrestrained. It felt so good to be out of that hotel room, out in the world, not worrying about what was going to happen between the two of them. Not analyzing every word and gesture. Just being. Tonight, they needed to have a serious discussion about what came next, because she could not go back to the way things were before. She couldn't pretend she didn't love him, nor could she go back to being just friends who worked together. It would kill her.

Suddenly, to her complete surprise and delight, Noah plopped into the snow beside her and together they made angels, moving their arms and legs in synchronized movements. For a moment, Hannah was stunned, watching him let go of his carefully maintained control, watching him be silly and carefree. But then she noticed he was deliberately moving closer to her, merging her snow angel with his, creating one joined impression in the snow.

"Hey, you're ruining the effect," Hannah cried, but she was laughing too hard to sound convincing.

"No," Noah said, turning his head to look at her, his blue eyes intense despite the playfulness of the moment. "We're making baby snow angels."

And then he kissed her, right there in the snow with families nearby and the world watching. His lips were cold against hers, almost numb from the frigid air, and yet Hannah suddenly felt so warm, heat flooding through her body, that she wanted to tear off her coat. But that would not be wise. That would be how people ended up in the ER with hypothermia.

When they came apart, she gazed into his sapphire eyes and smiled, feeling like her heart might burst. "This has been fun. This has been perfect."

"Yes," he agreed, "though I'm starting to get cold. I think my toes are ice cubes."

"We should go back," Hannah said and reached up and kissed him one last time, soft and sweet and full of promise.

He jumped up with surprising agility and then helped her to her feet, pulling her close for a moment before they began the process of wiping the snow from their clothes. Their fingers kept touching each other inappropriately, brushing against places they shouldn't in public, lingering longer than necessary, and they were laughing the entire time like teenagers on a first date.

Finally, hand in hand, they walked back to the jeep, and Hannah couldn't imagine them going back to being like they were before. She couldn't imagine sitting across from him in the break room and not touching him, working alongside him in the ER and not being able to kiss him, going home to her empty apartment when she wanted to go home to him. Yes, she enjoyed his friendship, treasured it, actually, but the last few days had confirmed her love for him beyond any doubt. She'd probably been in love with him for years, if she was being honest with herself. But now she knew her heart was fully involved, invested in a way it had never been before, and if they broke up, she'd be crushed.

Devastated.

Destroyed in ways she wasn't sure she could recover from.

Driving out of the parking spot, Noah traveled slowly, being cautious on the still-slick roads, and they were soon back at the hotel. The familiar building loomed before them, a haven from the cold.

"Let's visit the gift shop," Hannah suggested as they pulled into the parking lot. "Maybe they have something in there for your stepmother."

She knew he'd been worrying about finding her a present, that he wanted to make a good first impression on this woman who had made his father happy.

"All right," Noah agreed readily. "But I did bring her something small from home."

Oh good. Hannah wasn't certain he'd thought that far ahead. After all, this would be the first time they met, and first impressions mattered.

After they parked the jeep and walked inside, stamping snow from their boots, they were immediately confronted with a scene of chaos. A crowd of people stood around someone on the floor near the front desk, their voices raised in panic and concern. The woman they'd met on the elevator their first day, the one who'd been so friendly, was on her knees beside a man, crying hysterically.

"Ed, please honey, don't go," she sobbed, her voice breaking. "Please don't leave me. Stay with me."

Hannah felt her heart drop into her stomach. Not again.

Together, she and Noah rushed over to the man, their training overriding everything else, the playfulness of moments ago evaporating instantly.

"What's wrong? What happened?" Hannah asked, already assessing the situation with clinical eyes.

The woman looked up at them with a tear-stained face, mascara running down her cheeks. "He just dropped. We were checking out, and he grabbed his chest and fell to the floor. Oh God, please help him."

"Move back," Hannah commanded, her voice taking on the authoritative tone she used in the ER. "Everyone give us space. We're doctors. Has someone called 911?"

"Yes," a woman standing nearby said, her hands pressed to her mouth. "They're on their way."

Noah was already on his knees beside the man, his ear pressed to the man's chest, listening for a heartbeat, for breathing, for any sign of life.

"We need to start compressions," he said, looking up at Hannah, and she saw the determination in his eyes. "You take his mouth and I'll start compressions."

Hannah dropped to her knees beside the man's head and leaned down, tilting his chin back to open his airway. She pinched his nose closed and puffed two breaths into his mouth, watching to see if his chest rose. It did, slightly.

"Does the hotel have an AED machine?" Noah asked the gathering crowd, already starting compressions, his hands positioned correctly over the man's sternum. "An automated defibrillator?"

"No," a nervous desk clerk said, wringing his hands. "We don't. Should we? Oh God, we should have one."

They continued to work on him, Hannah giving breaths while Noah compressed the man's chest with steady, practiced movements. She counted silently, thirty compressions, two breaths, thirty compressions, two breaths, the rhythm as familiar as her own heartbeat.

Hannah heard the man's rib crack, a sound she'd heard too many times before, and saw Noah wince slightly. He had pressed just right, and the bone had broken under the force needed to circulate blood. But it was important not to stop, not to hesitate. A broken rib would heal. Death was permanent. And so they continued, working together seamlessly, a team.

The paramedics walked into the hotel, and Hannah had never been so relieved to see anyone in her life.

"Bring the defibrillator," Noah called out, not pausing in his compressions. "We need it now."

One man went back out to the ambulance while two others knelt beside them, opening their tactical kits.

"No pulse," Noah reported, slightly breathless from the exertion. "We started CPR about two minutes ago."

"How long has he been down total?" the lead paramedic asked, taking over compressions from Noah.

"Five minutes, maybe a little more," Noah said, sitting back on his heels. "You guys got here quick. Really quick."

"Good job," the paramedic said. "Only because we were less than a mile away, just cleared from another call."

The third paramedic returned with the defibrillator and quickly opened it, placing the pads on the man's chest.

"Clear," he called out loudly. "Everyone clear."

Everyone stopped working on the man and leaned away from him, hands up, ensuring they weren't touching him or anything touching him.

The machine analyzed his rhythm, then delivered a shock. The man's body jumped violently, his back arching off the floor.

Hannah leaned down automatically to give mouth-to-mouth again, but she felt him gasp beneath her, felt his chest expand on its own.

"He's breathing," she said, pulling back. "He's got a pulse. I can feel it."

"Oh, thank God," his wife sobbed. "Oh, thank you, thank you."

"Pulse is erratic," one paramedic said, his fingers on the man's wrist. "Irregular, but it's there. Let's get him to the hospital now. He needs a cath lab."

They brought the gurney in, and Hannah rose from the man, her knees protesting from kneeling on the hard floor. She went to his wife, who was trembling violently.

"He's doing better," Hannah said gently, putting a hand on the woman's shoulder. "He's still not out of the woods, he's going to need tests, but he's got a real chance now."

The woman threw her arms around Hannah, hugging her tight. "Thank you. Oh, thank you so much. What would we have done if you weren't here? What would I have done?"

Hannah would never tell the woman the truth, but without CPR, without immediate intervention, the man would have died. His heart had stopped, and without someone to manually pump blood to his brain and organs, he would have been gone within minutes. The paramedics had been close, but not close enough.

Without Hannah and Noah, this woman would be a widow right now.

The paramedics had him loaded onto the gurney, strapped in and ready to transport. The one who had been doing most of the talking smiled at them with recognition.

"You guys helped the lady who had fallen in the parking lot yesterday," he said, shaking his head in amazement. "And now, today, you saved this guy. Are we going to see you around here often?"

"No," Noah said, standing and brushing off his knees. "We're leaving tomorrow. Just as soon as the roads are officially opened."

"Well, safe travels," the paramedic said and hurried to catch up to his crew, pushing the gurney toward the door.

Hannah released the woman gently. "Ride in the ambulance. Go with them. Be with your husband."

"Thank you," the woman said again, her voice choked with tears, as she hurried after them.

With a sigh, Hannah shook her head and watched through the hotel's front windows as the ambulance drove away, lights flashing. People standing around began to disperse, the drama over, returning to their own lives and concerns. She glanced at Noah and saw something dark flicker across his face.

He took her hand without speaking, and they stepped onto the elevator together. The doors closed, sealing them in silence.

"This is beginning to feel like work," Hannah said, trying to lighten the mood, trying to shake off the adrenaline still coursing through her system. "Maybe we should bill the hotel."

"Yes," he replied shortly, his jaw tight.

Hannah replayed the scene in her mind, running through their actions, and something occurred to her. "You broke the guy's rib," she said, not thinking anything negative about what he'd done. It happened sometimes during CPR. When you were doing proper compressions with enough force to actually circulate blood, it was easy to break a rib, especially in older patients.

It was unfortunate but often unavoidable. She'd done it herself more than once.

She felt Noah tense beside her, his hand tightening around hers almost painfully as they reached their floor and stepped off the elevator.

They walked down the hall in silence, and Hannah felt a growing sense of unease. Something was wrong. Something had shifted.

Noah opened the door with jerky movements, and they stepped inside. As soon as they were inside and the door closed behind them, he turned to face her, and Hannah saw anger in his eyes, real anger that shocked her.

"Yes, I broke the man's rib, but I saved his life," he said, his voice sharp and defensive. "Don't ever question what I do again."

What the hell had just happened? Why was he acting this way? Hannah felt like she'd been slapped. It wasn't like she didn't think he'd done a good job, he'd been perfect, professional, had done everything exactly right. She'd just made a simple statement, an observation, the kind of thing they said to each other all the time at work.

"I wasn't questioning your decision," Hannah said carefully, trying to understand where this was coming from. "I was merely making an observation. It happens. You know it happens."

"Well, don't," he said coldly. "Just don't."

Stunned, Hannah stared at him, feeling the warmth and joy from the park evaporating like snow in sunshine. He'd never acted this way before, never snapped at her, never been defensive about his medical skills, never looked at her with that expression on his face. And she didn't appreciate what he was doing now. They were supposed to be partners. They were supposed to trust each other.

Why was he acting like this? What had she done to trigger such an extreme reaction?

And suddenly, Hannah felt the fragile happiness of the morning shatter into pieces around her feet.

CHAPTER 12

In practice together, his parents had made his life miserable with their constant disagreements, their endless battles over treatment protocols and patient care decisions, until finally, his mother had dissolved the practice and gone out on her own. She'd walked away from everything, the business they'd built together, the life they'd shared, the marriage they'd promised would last forever. She'd walked away from him and his father, and to this day, Noah felt the abandonment like a physical wound that had never quite healed, that still ached when he prodded it.

It was one thing to end their professional partnership, to decide they couldn't work together anymore. But it was quite another thing entirely to leave her child and husband, to pack her bags and move across town, and act like they were strangers when they passed on the street. Thank goodness Noah had been in high school by then, old enough to understand what was happening, old enough to know that he was going to college and eventually to medical school regardless of what his mother did. Old enough to survive, even if he wasn't old enough to understand why she'd chosen her career over her family.

And he'd made the decision right then, standing in his empty childhood home watching his father cry at the kitchen table, that he would never get involved with another doctor. Never mix his professional and personal life. Never risk experiencing that kind of pain again. And yet Hannah was his best friend, his closest confidant, the person he trusted most in the world. How had he let this happen?

Today, in that elevator, she'd done exactly what his mother used to do to his father. She'd pointed out a mistake, no, not even a mistake, just an unfortunate consequence of doing his job correctly, and Noah could see it all playing out again. He could see the anger in Hannah's expression, or at least he thought he could, and suddenly all his doubts regarding the two of them working together and then living together came crashing down on him like an avalanche, burying him in fear and panic.

He would never return to the horror of what he'd witnessed growing up. Never. Two adults screaming at one another because they shared the same profession and didn't always agree on the best course of treatment. Two people who supposedly loved each other tearing each other apart over medical decisions that, in the grand scheme of things, didn't matter half as much as their relationship should have.

Yes, his mother had mental health issues, Noah could acknowledge that now, could recognize the signs of her untreated bipolar disorder, her refusal to take medication because she claimed it dulled her mind. But most of the time she had been normal, functional, even loving. Except when it came to his father, who seemed to trigger her worst episodes without even trying. His father's mere presence could set her off, could send her spiraling into rage or despair.

Strange that as a boy, Noah had learned when to avoid her and what not to say to trigger an outburst. He'd become an expert at reading her moods, at knowing when to make himself scarce, at understanding which topics were safe and which would lead to explosions. What kind of childhood was that? What kind of life had he lived, walking on eggshells in his own home?

But he would never live through that kind of situation again. Never subject himself to that kind of emotional warfare. Never put himself in a position where someone he loved could hurt him that deeply.

"I can't do this," Noah said, the words coming out harsher than he'd intended.

Hannah's face crumbled, and Noah felt something twist in his chest at the sight of her pain. "All because I made an observation?" she asked, her voice small and confused. "I didn't say you did anything wrong, Noah. It's common when you do CPR to break a patient's rib. I've done it myself. I'm kind of at a loss as to what is going on here. Why are you acting this way?"

"We work together," Noah said, trying to explain what he could barely explain to himself. "And I promised myself years ago that I'd never get involved with anyone I work with. I swore I wouldn't make that mistake. And yet for the last three days, we've been fucking like rabbits and becoming more than friends, and I've let myself forget why I made that promise in the first place."

She nodded slowly, processing his words. "What does that have to do with me telling you that you broke the man's rib? I'm so confused, Noah. I'm trying to understand, but I don't know what you're angry about."

"This could ruin our friendship," Noah said desperately. "Don't you see? This thing between us could destroy everything we've built over the years."

"I agree," Hannah said carefully. "But it could also be the best thing that's ever happened to us. You asked me to come with you on this trip because you were uncertain about how to handle the fact that your father had remarried. You wanted me to pretend to be your fiancée to make things easier, to avoid questions, to have someone by your side. Why are you lying to them? Why are you asking me to do this when I have wanted to be your girlfriend for years? Everything was going great between us until I said something you didn't like. That's never happened before when I disagreed with you about something medical. We've had different opinions on cases dozens of times, and you've never reacted like this."

Noah's chest seized, tightening until he could barely breathe. That moment on the elevator had reminded him too vividly of his parents, of watching them destroy each other over the course of years. Of how they'd ruined their relationship because they worked together, because they couldn't separate their professional disagreements from their personal lives. Of the arguments they'd had over the smallest things, a misdiagnosis, a treatment choice, a patient complaint. Of how his mother had criticized his father constantly, relentlessly, for his work as a doctor, as a parent, and even as a lover. Nothing he did was ever good enough. Nothing could satisfy her.

Would this be how it would eventually become with Hannah? Would they start out happy and in love, only to have their careers poison everything good between them? Would she start to resent him, to criticize him, to pick apart every decision he made until there was nothing left but bitterness and regret?

Going to meet his father and new stepmother, Noah had needed Hannah's presence beside him, helping him to stay calm and not let his emotions take over. He'd needed her steady support, her familiar warmth, her ability to make him laugh when everything felt too serious. Yes, he'd asked her to be his fake fiancée, but he hadn't truly understood her feelings at the time. He'd been willfully blind to what was right in front of him.

All he'd known was that he wanted to avoid awkward questions about when he was going to settle down, whether he was seeing anyone, why he was still single at his age. The fake engagement had seemed like a brilliant solution, a way to deflect attention and make the visit easier. But sometimes even a smart man had spectacularly stupid ideas, and this had been one of his worst.

Oh hell, he'd been avoiding recognizing the emotions that had been growing subtly between them for years. He'd known Hannah wanted more, and he'd deliberately ignored it, pushed it aside, pretended not to notice the way she looked at him or the hope in her eyes when they spent time together. He'd been afraid, and today his worst fears were being realized right before his eyes.

"I'm afraid, Hannah," Noah admitted, the words feeling like they were being torn from somewhere deep inside him. "I'm terrified of our jobs tearing us apart like it did my adoptive parents. My mother criticized my father all the time for the decisions he made regarding his patients. She would scream at him that he was incompetent, that he was going to get sued, that he was a disgrace to the profession. And if you were to scream at me like that, shouting that I was an idiot, or if you were to run out of the house and leave like she did, it would wreck me. It would destroy me completely. I can't do this. I promised myself as a young man that I would never marry anyone who was in the same profession as me, and I meant it."

Hannah turned to face him fully, and Noah could see the pain and frustration warring in her expression. She sighed deeply, a sound full of resignation and sadness.

"You think I would do that to you?" she asked quietly. "Noah, I didn't criticize you on the elevator. I stated a fact and didn't make a judgment call about your abilities or your decisions. You're the one who's upset about this. To me, it was nothing, just a clinical observation, the kind we make to each other every single day at work. I'm not your mother, Noah. We're not your parents. How we create our relationship is between us and has nothing to do with them or their dysfunction."

"But you don't understand," Noah insisted, wishing desperately that she could see his point, that she could understand the terror that gripped him. "They worked together. They were partners. And look how badly it turned out. Look at the carnage they left behind."

He could still remember so many specific fights, could still hear his mother's voice echoing through their house late at night. Could still remember hiding in his room with his hands over his ears, trying to block out the sound of his parents destroying each other with words.

Hannah walked up close to him, close enough that he could smell her familiar vanilla scent, see the determination in her green eyes.

"I've never screamed at you," she said firmly. "Not once in all the years we've known each other. But that doesn't mean that I'm not going to let you know my opinion when I have one. We're not always going to agree on everything, no two people do. But I will never engage in screaming matches with you. If we were to marry and have children, they would never see or hear us fight the way you witnessed with your parents. We may have heated discussions that we will take to the bedroom, away from them, where we can talk things through like adults. But I'm not raising children in a hostile environment, and that's what it sounds like you were raised in as a child."

She was right. God, she was absolutely right. And yet Noah couldn't seem to let go of his fear, couldn't seem to move past the terror that had been programmed into him over years of witnessing his parents' toxic relationship.

What could he say? He'd made up his mind. This could go no further. It was safer to stop now, before things got too complicated, before they hurt each other too badly to recover.

"We need to return to being friends," Noah said quietly, even though the words tasted like ash in his mouth. "Today showed me that we cannot work and live together. It's not going to work."

Hannah's face tightened, every muscle going rigid, and then she walked deliberately to the door. Her movements were controlled, measured, but Noah could see the emotion roiling beneath the surface.

"That's fine," she said, and her voice was steady despite the tears he could see forming in her eyes. "I can't do this anymore, Noah. I've ignored my feelings for years, pushed them aside, told myself that being your friend was enough. Just as soon as this storm passes, I'm going to catch a flight home to Houston. I'm not going to your father's house with you. I need to make a clean break. And that begins just as soon as humanly possible."

This was just like his parents, Noah thought with growing horror. Except that there had not been a clean break at all with them. It had been building for years, festering, getting worse and worse until the final explosion. And then it had been messy and painful and traumatic, with him and his father receiving most of the collateral damage from his mother's departure. And then when she had committed suicide eight years later, it had been devastating in ways Noah still hadn't fully processed. He often felt like he'd failed her, like he should have seen the signs, should have done something to save her.

"Hannah, don't you see you're doing exactly what my mother did?" Noah said desperately. "You're leaving. You're walking away."

"No, I'm not," Hannah said sharply, her patience clearly wearing thin. "I'm not screaming at you. I'm not being mean or hateful or vindictive. I'm not criticizing you or tearing you down. There's no point in any of that. You don't love me, Noah, and I need someone who is going to love me and want to spend forever with me. I actually liked the fact that we had the same occupation. I loved talking medicine with you, debating cases, and learning from you. For years, you've been my support system, my rock, but I need more than that. I need a partner, not just a friend."

Standing there, feeling like the ground was crumbling beneath his feet, all Noah could think about was that he didn't want her to end their friendship. And the truth, the terrifying, vulnerable truth, was that he did love her. He'd loved her for years, had been in love with her probably since the first year they'd worked together. But he was so afraid. So paralyzed by fear that he couldn't seem to move forward, couldn't seem to take the risk.

"I want a husband and family," Hannah continued, her voice breaking slightly on the words. "I want forever with someone. I want my husband to be my best friend, the one I always turn to no matter what happens, and I thought you might be him. I really did. But, obviously, you don't feel the same way. So I'll be leaving as soon as I can book a flight."

No, this could not be happening. This couldn't be how things ended between them. Yes, Noah understood what she was saying. He understood that he was the problem here. Not her. Never her. It was all him and his baggage and his inability to move past his childhood trauma.

"Can we please walk back from the edge here and just remain friends?" Noah asked, hearing the desperation in his own voice and hating it. He was hoping for reconciliation, for some way to fix this, but doubting there was any chance of salvaging what they'd had.

Hannah looked at him for a long moment, and Noah could see the exact moment when something shifted in her eyes, when she made her decision.

"You've had over five years of my life to figure out if I was the woman for you," she said quietly. "Five years, Noah. And one comment, one simple, innocent comment about a broken rib, has sent you spiraling. There is no way we can continue as friends or lovers after this. You've shown me exactly how you see me, how you see us. As soon as this storm clears, I'm going back to Houston. But I won't be there when you return. It's time for me to go home to my family in Oklahoma. It's time for me to start over somewhere new. I thought we had something special, but you've got serious issues you haven't dealt with. And I'm no longer the girl who will wait around for you to figure them out. I deserve better than that."

Noah didn't like the sound of that, any of it. And yet, he couldn't blame her. He couldn't argue with her logic or her right to want more from life. She deserved someone who could give her everything she wanted. She deserved someone who wasn't broken.

He was filled with so much fear, so much panic, that he could barely think straight. But underneath all of that, underneath the terror and the trauma responses, there was something else. A small voice that was getting louder, that was telling him he was making the biggest mistake of his life.

He was losing her. He was losing the best thing that had ever happened to him. And it was entirely his own fault.

Noah opened his mouth to say something, anything, to stop her from walking out that door. But the words wouldn't come. The fear was too strong, the old patterns too deeply ingrained. And so he stood there, frozen, watching as Hannah picked up her phone and began searching for flights home.

Watching as the woman he loved slipped through his fingers like snow melting in the sun.

And knowing that he had no one to blame but himself.

CHAPTER 13

The next morning, Hannah walked out of the honeymoon suite, determined never to look back, her shoulders squared and her head held high, even though everything inside her was crumbling. Tears filled her eyes, blurring her vision as she pulled her suitcase behind her down the carpeted hallway. Yet, she remained unwavering in her resolve not to let her emotions sway her from what needed to be done. Time to look out for herself for once. Time to stop waiting for someone else to choose her. Time to make her dreams come true, even if those dreams no longer included the man she'd thought would be part of them forever.

With a heavy heart that felt like it weighed a thousand pounds, closing the door on Noah Baker and everything they could have been.

She didn't look back. If she looked back, she might lose her resolve. If she looked back, she might see him standing there, might let herself hope he'd changed his mind, might give him another chance to break her heart.

On her way to the elevator, dragging her suitcase and blinking back tears that refused to stop forming, Hannah ran into

119

the woman whose husband she and Noah had saved just yester-day. The woman's face lit up when she saw Hannah, and before Hannah could say anything, before she could prepare herself, the woman grabbed her and pulled her into a huge, enthusiastic hug.

"Ralph is doing so well," the woman gushed, her voice filled with joy and gratitude. "The doctors say he's going to make a full recovery. You guys saved his life, and I can't ever thank you enough. You're both heroes. Absolute heroes."

The very thing that had torn them apart, their shared profes-sion, their ability to work together seamlessly, their medical skills that complemented each other so perfectly, and this woman was thanking her for it. The irony wasn't lost on Hannah. But she would do it again in a heartbeat, would save Ralph's life a hundred times over, even knowing what it had cost her.

"I'm so glad to hear he's doing better," Hannah said, trying to inject warmth into her voice despite the ice spreading through her chest. "We were just doing our job. Any doctor would have done the same."

"Well, you saved my sweetheart, and I know how you two lovebirds feel about one another," the woman said, smiling with such genuine happiness that it made Hannah want to cry even harder. "Anyone could see the love between you two. I'm going to get some rest, I haven't slept in almost forty-eight hours, and then later, I would love to take you two to dinner. My treat. It's the least I can do."

There was no way Hannah could sit through a dinner with Noah, pretending everything was fine, making small talk while her heart was shattering into smaller and smaller pieces. There was no way she could look at him across a table and not remember everything they'd shared, everything they'd lost.

"That's not necessary, really," Hannah said, forcing a smile that felt like it might crack her face. "I've got a plane to catch. Noah is leaving today as well."

She couldn't bring herself to tell this kind woman the truth, that as of last night, she and Noah were no longer officially fake-engaged, no longer best friends, no longer even friends at all. That everything had fallen apart in the span of a single conversation. That the man she loved was too broken to love her back.

Hannah was on her way home, where she would give her notice to the Houston hospital where they worked, pack up her life there, and return to Oklahoma City, where her family was, where she could get a position at any hospital she wanted. Where her family would surround her with their love and support and help heal her wounded heart, even if it took years.

"It's a lovely idea, but your focus should be on taking care of Ralph right now," Hannah said gently. "Are your children nearby? Will they be able to come see him?"

"Just as soon as the roads clear completely, they'll be here," the woman said, her eyes bright with tears of relief and joy. "They're driving in from Seattle and Denver."

Hannah grabbed the woman's hand and squeezed it, one last human connection before she walked away from this place and these memories forever. "Have a wonderful Christmas with your family. Tell Ralph I'm glad he's okay."

"Thank you, dear," the woman said warmly. "You too. Have a wonderful Christmas with your young man."

Hannah just smiled and nodded, not trusting herself to speak, not wanting to shatter this woman's happiness with the truth of her own misery.

Hannah would be spending the holiday alone at home in Texas. Completely alone. She was on a noon flight and should be back in Houston by tonight if the connections worked out. She'd pick up something to eat, probably something unhealthy and comforting that she could eat straight from the container while sitting on her couch, and just hibernate for a few days. Maybe even start packing up her apartment, sorting through the remnants of a life she'd built in Houston, a life that had revolved so much around Noah. As much as she hated to leave the city, hated to uproot herself again, it was for the best. She couldn't work with him anymore. Couldn't see him every day and pretend her heart wasn't broken. Couldn't watch him move on with his life while she remained stuck in place.

Hannah waved goodbye to the woman and then stepped onto the elevator, her finger hovering over the lobby button for just a moment. Time to go. This trip had given her all the knowledge she needed, had shown her exactly where she stood, exactly what Noah was capable of giving, exactly how little that was compared to what she deserved. And now she had to deal with the heartache, had to process the grief, had to somehow move forward. But she was a strong woman. She'd survived worse. She knew what needed to be done.

Erase Noah Baker from her life forever.

Delete his number from her phone. Unfriend him on social media. Avoid the break room at work until she could give her notice. Pack up every memory, every gift, every photograph, and put it all away where she'd never have to see it again.

It sounded so simple. So clean. So final.

So why did it feel like she was dying inside?

Thirty minutes later, after checking out of the hotel and catching a shuttle through the now-cleared roads, Hannah was in the airport once again, sitting in the same terminal where she'd arrived just days ago, full of hope and nervous excitement. Waiting for her flight home. Waiting for this nightmare to end.

The airport was crowded with people who'd been stranded by the storm, all of them eager to get home, to get back to their lives. Families reuniting, business travelers looking exhausted, couples holding hands. Everyone seemed to have somewhere to be, someone waiting for them.

Hannah had never felt more alone.

She bought a paperback novel from the small bookstore, some romance that promised a happily ever after she no longer believed in, and a large cup of coffee that she didn't really want but bought anyway because she needed something to do with her hands. Then she found a relatively comfortable chair near her gate, tucked herself into the corner, and tried to disappear.

Only two and a half hours until her flight. Only two and a half hours until this part of her life was over. Only two and a half hours until she could start pretending that the last three days had never happened.

Her chest physically ached from losing Noah, a sharp pain beneath her breastbone that wouldn't go away no matter how many deep breaths she took. They'd been so close for so long, five years of friendship, of trust, of understanding each other in ways no one else did. Five years of inside jokes and shared traumas and late-night conversations about everything and nothing. Five years of her falling deeper and deeper in love while he remained carefully distant, always keeping part of himself locked away where she couldn't reach.

But no more. It was over and she would carry on without him. Somehow. Eventually. When the pain wasn't quite so fresh and raw.

Opening the novel with trembling fingers, Hannah read the first three pages five times, and each time the words refused to make sense, refused to form a coherent narrative. Each time, a tear dropped onto the page, blurring the ink, making it impossible to focus. Damn him. Damn Noah Baker for making her fall in love with him. Damn him for being exactly what she wanted and then refusing to let her have him. Damn him for making the wrong choice when the right one was standing right in front of him.

She was worthy. She was deserving. She was enough. They had been perfect for one another, everyone could see it, everyone except Noah himself. Until now, until last night's devastating conversation, Hannah had never fully realized how badly damaged Noah was from his childhood. She'd known his family life wasn't ideal, had known there was divorce and trauma and complications. But he'd never told her the details. Never told her about the screaming that had filled his childhood home. The constant fighting between his parents. The way they had criticized and torn each other down over medical decisions. The way they had made him distrust everything, relationships, partnerships, love itself.

And yet he'd always trusted her before until yesterday. Until one innocent comment about a broken rib had triggered something in him, had sent him spiraling back into his worst fears, had made him see her as the enemy instead of his partner.

Glancing at her watch, wiping at her eyes with the back of her hand, Hannah realized there was still well over an hour before boarding would begin. Well over an hour of sitting here with nothing to distract her from her thoughts, from the memories that kept playing on repeat in her mind. The snowman they'd built. The snow angels merged together. The way he'd looked at her when they made love. The way he'd held her afterward, like he never wanted to let go.

All of it meant nothing now.

Once she left this snow-drenched land, she'd be glad. She'd be relieved. She'd be able to start moving on. That's what she told herself, anyway, even though she knew it was a lie. She'd miss Montana. She'd miss the beauty of it, the pristine white landscape, the way the mountains looked in the distance. She'd miss what this trip could have been, meeting Noah's father, spending Christmas together, taking the next step in their relationship.

But mostly she'd miss the version of Noah she'd seen here, the one who'd laughed in the snow, who'd built a snowman with her, who'd made love to her like she was precious. The Noah who'd almost let himself be happy.

This morning, she'd awakened to the sun shining brightly into the honeymoon suite, streaming through the windows and illuminating the room with golden light. The storm had passed. The skies had cleared. Everything outside looked fresh, new, and hopeful.

Everything inside Hannah felt dead and grey.

If Noah heard her leave, heard her moving quietly around the room, packing her things, wheeling her suitcase to the door, he hadn't said a word. Hadn't tried to stop her. Hadn't asked her to stay. In fact, they had barely spoken all night long after their argument. They'd existed in the same space like strangers, like two people who'd never meant anything to each other at all. And that was for the best, Hannah told herself. Clean breaks healed faster, or so people said. Though Hannah had her doubts about whether this particular wound would ever truly heal.

There was nothing left to say. Nothing left to go over. They'd said it all yesterday afternoon in that hotel room. It had been abundantly clear that Noah's mind was made up, that he believed he'd made a terrible mistake by sleeping with her, by letting himself get close, by allowing their friendship to become something more. He'd retreated behind his walls and locked the door, and Hannah didn't have the key. She wasn't even sure one existed.

Noah didn't love her enough to overcome his fears of them working together. He didn't love her enough to believe they could be different from his parents. He didn't love her enough to take a chance, to be brave, to choose her over his trauma.

And she wasn't going to give up being a doctor for him or for anyone else. That wasn't possible. That wasn't even something she'd consider. She'd worked too long and too hard to get where she was, had sacrificed too much, had dreamed of this career since she was a little girl. Being a doctor wasn't just what she did, it was who she was. And if Noah couldn't accept that, couldn't see that their shared profession could be a strength rather than a weakness, then there was no future for them.

Now she knew the truth, and it was time for her to pick up the pieces of her shattered heart and move on. Time to go home and start her life over from scratch. Time to begin again without her best friend by her side. Time to return home to Oklahoma City, where she'd grown up, where her parents and siblings still lived, where she could rebuild herself in familiar surroundings.

Time to accept that sometimes love wasn't enough.

Hannah closed the book she wasn't reading and stared out the window at the planes taking off and landing, at people arriving and departing, at lives intersecting and separating. Somewhere out there, Noah was probably on his way to Whitefish to see his father. Probably relieved she was gone. Probably already compartmentalizing what had happened between them, filing it away under "mistakes" and moving on with his carefully controlled life.

She wondered if he'd miss her. Wondered if he'd regret his choice. Wondered if someday, maybe years from now, he'd realize what he'd given up.

But it didn't matter. Even if he did regret it, even if he came crawling back, Hannah knew she couldn't do this again. Couldn't put herself through this pain again. Couldn't be with someone who saw loving her as a risk instead of a gift.

She deserved better than that.

She deserved someone who would choose her. Every single time.

The announcement came over the loudspeaker that her flight would begin boarding in twenty minutes. Hannah gathered her things, the unread book, the cold coffee, her purse, her carry-on, and stood up, straightening her spine, forcing herself to breathe.

Twenty minutes until she left Montana.

Twenty minutes until she left Noah Baker behind forever.

She could do this. She was strong enough. She had to be.

Even if right now, sitting in this airport with tears streaming down her face that she couldn't seem to stop, she felt like the weakest person in the world.

CHAPTER 14

When Noah awoke, the sun was streaming through the windows of the honeymoon suite, bright and cheerful and mocking. The snow had stopped. The storm had passed. Everything outside looked fresh and clean and new, like the world had been given a second chance.

Unlike Noah.

His hand reached over to the other side of the bed automatically, seeking Hannah's warmth, and he realized with a jolt of panic that it was empty. Cold. She'd been gone for a while.

Sitting straight up, his heart already pounding with dread, Noah gazed frantically about the room. Everything looked wrong. The air felt different. Empty.

Her clothes were no longer hanging in the closet. The side she'd used was bare, the hangers swaying slightly as if she'd just ripped her things down in a hurry. Jumping up, still in his boxers, Noah ran into the bathroom to find her toiletries were gone, her toothbrush, her makeup bag, that vanilla lotion that had driven him crazy for three days. All of it vanished like she'd never been there at all.

"No, no, no," Noah muttered, yanking out his phone with shaking hands.

He called her and reached her voicemail almost immediately. The sound of her voice, bright and professional, made his chest constrict painfully.

"Hannah, call me," Noah said, trying to keep his voice steady and failing miserably. "Please. We need to talk. I was wrong. God, Hannah, I was so wrong. Please call me back."

He ended the call and stared at his phone, willing it to ring. Nothing.

The room was eerily silent except for the sound of plows clearing the streets outside, their engines rumbling and scraping against pavement. But where was Hannah? How long had she been gone? Had she taken a taxi to the airport? Was she already on a plane?

The thought made Noah's stomach drop sickeningly.

He texted her with fumbling fingers: "Call me. Please. I'm sorry."

Nothing. No response. No indication that she'd even read it.

He sent another: "Hannah, I love you. Please don't leave."

Still nothing.

Glancing around the room wildly, Noah felt panic rising in his throat like bile. He wanted to get out on the road immediately, wanted to chase after her, but it was still early. They were still clearing the roads and the highway would take a long time, hours, probably. The main routes would be prioritized, but it would still be slow going.

After getting dressed in a frenzy, not caring that his shirt was inside out until he caught sight of himself in the mirror and had to fix it, Noah packed up his belongings, shoving things haphazardly into his suitcase. Then he grabbed his laptop and checked the airline schedule with trembling hands.

There was a flight to Denver and then connecting on to

Houston leaving at noon. Could she be on that flight? It was the most logical choice. The earliest option to get home.

Still no text or call from Hannah. His phone remained stubbornly silent, taunting him.

Had he been wrong when he'd ended their relationship? The question pounded in his head like a drum. Of course, he'd been wrong. He knew that now, he could see it with painful clarity in the harsh light of morning. Had he been catastrophically wrong when he'd gotten upset over something as stupid as her mentioning he'd broken the man's rib? Yes. God, yes. It was true, he'd heard the rib crack and winced at the sound, felt that familiar pang of regret even though he knew it was necessary, unavoidable. But the man was hopefully alive right now, breathing, talking to his family, getting the medical care he needed. Noah had saved his life. They had saved his life together.

And he'd punished Hannah for being there, for being his partner, for doing exactly what a good doctor should do.

Noah sat on the edge of the bed, his head in his hands. What had he done? What the hell had he done?

He called his father, needing guidance, needing someone to tell him he wasn't as much of an idiot as he felt like.

"Son," his father answered on the second ring, sounding cheerful and well-rested. "Are you getting ready to leave? The roads should be clear by mid-morning."

"Not yet," Noah said, his voice hoarse. "I hear the snow plows clearing the roads, and I want to give them time to get the highway done properly. But we'll be there later today. Hopefully."

"Is everything all right?" his father asked, and Noah could hear the concern creeping into his voice. "You don't sound like yourself."

Could his father hear the distress in his voice? The barely controlled panic? Hannah was gone, and she wouldn't return his calls or texts, and he was entirely to blame. The thought of her leaving Houston and returning to Oklahoma, of never seeing her again, of losing her forever, made his heart pound so hard in his chest he thought it might explode. Made his hands shake and his vision blur and his breathing come too fast.

What did he say to his father? And would his father be able to help him understand what he should do now? The man had remarried and seemed very happy with his new wife. Was Noah wrong not to want to work with the person he loved? Or was that just another excuse, another way of protecting himself from getting hurt?

"Hannah left me," Noah said bluntly, the words tasting like ash in his mouth.

"What do you mean she left you?" his father asked, confusion evident. "Where did she go?"

"We saved a man yesterday who was having a heart attack in the hotel lobby," Noah explained, the words tumbling out. "While doing CPR, I broke his rib. She mentioned it to me in the elevator afterward. Nothing derogatory, nothing critical, just a simple statement of fact, and I reacted badly. I reacted like Mom used to react to you when you'd done something she didn't approve of. I accused her of criticizing me, of questioning my abilities. And I was so wrong, Dad. I was so completely wrong."

There was silence on the other end of the line for a long moment, and Noah could almost hear his father processing this information.

"So the fake engagement is real?," his father said carefully.

"How did you know?"

His father laughed. "That girl has been crazy about you for a long time, but you're the one who wasn't ready to commit."

Even his own father had known that Hannah loved him. Had seen the sparks between them.

"That was the other thing that happened this weekend," Noah admitted, feeling like he was confessing his sins. "She told me she's had feelings for me for a while now, years, actually. But she's tired of waiting for me to catch up, tired of putting her life on hold while I figure out what I want. She said it was time for her to move on if I didn't reciprocate her feelings."

"Do you have feelings for her?" his father asked gently.

This was the hard part. Did Noah dare admit how he felt about her after everything that had happened? After they'd had sex for three days straight? After he'd held her and made love to her and felt more connected to another human being than he'd ever felt in his entire life? Yes, he loved her desperately. But should he tell his father? Should he admit it out loud and make it real?

"Yes," Noah said, his voice breaking. "I've loved her for a long time, years, probably. But I always thought back to you and Mother and the way you fought constantly over your medical practice, over patients, over every little decision. I don't want that to happen to us. I couldn't survive it. And when Hannah said I broke the man's rib, I just... I automatically assumed we were heading down that same path."

"You automatically assumed you two were going to be like me and Francis," his father said, understanding dawning in his voice.

"Yes, Dad," Noah said, knowing with crushing certainty that he'd been wrong, that he'd overreacted, that he'd destroyed the best thing in his life over his own irrational fears. His head was telling him he'd catastrophically overreacted while his heart was calling him every kind of fool that existed.

"So how is she today?" his father asked.

That was the worst part. The part that made Noah feel like he couldn't breathe.

"When I woke up this morning, she was gone," Noah said, his voice hollow. "Her clothes, her things, everything. She didn't leave a note. She won't answer my calls. What do I do, Dad? I don't want us to become like you and Mom. I don't want to scream at each other or fight about work or let our careers destroy what we have. But more than that, so much more than that, I don't want to lose her. I love her, and now I'm going to have to face life without her, and I don't know how to do that."

"Is that what you want?" his father asked quietly.

"No," Noah said, and it came out like a wail, like the cry of a wounded animal. "I don't want to lose her. I can't lose her."

"You want to be able to have your cake and eat it too," his father said, not unkindly but with the bluntness of someone who'd lived long enough to recognize the truth. "You want to have your friend, your lover, your partner, but not make any lasting commitments because what if you and her became like me and Francis? What if you end up broken and divorced and damaged like we were?"

While Noah hated to admit it, that was exactly his fear. That was the nightmare that had haunted him for years. And coming from his father, hearing it stated so plainly, it sounded so stupid. So childish. So completely irrational.

Hannah did not have a mental health problem like his mother had. She was not psychotic or unstable or prone to violent mood swings. She didn't have episodes of paranoia or depression or act anything like his mother had acted. Hannah was steady, rational, kind, brilliant. Hannah was everything his mother hadn't been.

"Yes," Noah admitted, his voice small. "That's exactly what I'm afraid of."

Why couldn't they just be friends with benefits or something like that? Something safe and controlled and without the risk of devastating loss? But even as he thought it, Noah knew how ridiculous that sounded. You couldn't put love in a box and expect it to stay there.

His father sighed deeply. "Son, you and Hannah are not me and Francis. You're not doomed to repeat our mistakes."

Isn't that what Hannah had said? Hadn't those been almost her exact words?

"In fact," his father continued, "I doubt any doctor you married would act like we did when you were a child. I'm sorry you had to witness that, sorry we put you through that. But your mother was diagnosed with schizophrenia right after we married. It was one of the reasons she refused to get pregnant initially, why we had to adopt you. Does Hannah have schizophrenia?"

Noah felt like he'd been punched in the gut. "What? I didn't know that. I knew she had issues, but I didn't know it was schizophrenia."

"There's a lot you don't know, son. A lot we need to talk about."

"No," Noah said, answering his father's question. "Hannah doesn't have schizophrenia. She's logical, thorough, and rational. She's the best damn doctor I know. She's the best person I know."

"Then what makes you think she would act like your mother?" his father pressed. "What makes you think she would scream and yell at you like your mother did to me? What makes you think loving her is a risk instead of a gift?"

For a moment, Noah sat in silence, remembering what Hannah had said about screaming at him. Her voice echoed in his memory: "I've never screamed at you. I will never engage in screaming matches with you. We're not your parents."

Sitting on the bed, Noah glanced around the hotel room. It seemed so empty now, so silent, and yet it echoed with her words, with her presence, with the ghost of what they'd shared here. He was so damn stupid. Not because of what Hannah had said, she'd been right about everything. But because he'd let his past dictate his future. Because he'd been so terrified of becoming his parents that he'd sabotaged the one relationship that could have saved him from their fate.

She was not his mother. She was Hannah. A better doctor, a better person, he'd never met.

"Son?" his father prompted. "Are you still there?"

"Oh, Dad," Noah said, his voice breaking as tears finally spilled down his cheeks. "I've royally screwed this up. I've destroyed everything. She was right there, loving me, wanting to be with me, and I pushed her away because I was too afraid to be happy."

His heart was breaking into a thousand shards inside his chest. He'd fucked up everything. And now because of him, Christmas would be totally ruined. Hannah would be alone. He would be alone, even surrounded by family. They would both be miserable because he'd been too much of a coward to fight for what they had.

"Son, I've been waiting for years for you to realize that you and Hannah were perfect for one another," his father said gently. "And now I understand why you've not put a ring on that girl's finger. You've been terrified. But she is not your mother, Noah. She's a rational human being who does not have mental health issues. Your mother had all kinds of problems, severe, untreated problems, and spent a month in a psychiatric hospital when I came home one day and found her giving you tranquilizers to calm you down. After that, we made a deal that she had no access to any drugs in the house. I should have talked to you about this years ago. I should have explained everything. I'm sorry I didn't."

Stunned, Noah stared out at the sunshine streaming through the windows, trying to process this information. "Mother gave me tranquilizers? When I was a kid?"

"Yes," his father sighed heavily. "You were maybe five or six. She wanted to calm you down because you were a rambunctious, energetic kid, and she was older, struggling with her illness. When I found out what she'd been doing, I stopped it immediately and insisted she get help. There is so much we need to talk about when you get here. We're going to have a very frank discussion about your life, about where you came from, about things I should have told you years ago."

That sounded ominous. Was his father going to tell him about his birth parents? About his adoption? About other secrets the family had kept?

"What else haven't you told me?" Noah asked.

"We'll talk when you get here," his father said. "But right now, what's important is this: I never thought our fighting would hurt you so badly. I never realized the damage we were doing. Most people talk and work out their problems calmly, rationally. Your mother thought screaming was the answer to everything. Maybe she learned it from her parents, I don't know. But just remember this, son: Love can solve most problems if you let it. Now you need to go find Hannah and work this out between you. If you love her, then you need to tell her, need to fight for her, or you're going to lose her forever. And trust me when I say that living with that kind of regret will destroy you."

Seeing clearly for the first time in years, maybe for the first time in his entire life, Noah planned his next actions with the precision of a surgeon. "You're right, Dad. You're absolutely right. Thanks for being honest with me. We'll see you soon. Love you."

"We're looking forward to you being here," his father said warmly. "Be careful on those roads. I love you and I hope you work things out with Hannah. I really do."

"Me too," Noah said as he disconnected the line, already moving, already grabbing his things.

He'd bet anything Hannah was at the airport right now, waiting for that noon flight, probably crying and hating him and planning her escape from Houston. From him. From everything they could have been.

Now he needed to get there and somehow convince her he'd made a stupid, terrible mistake. He needed to tell her that stupid mistake had taught him so much, about himself, about his parents' disastrous marriage, about what real love looked like versus the toxic relationship he'd grown up witnessing. His father had said he had other things he needed to tell Noah, secrets that needed to come out. What could that be about? His adoption? His birth parents? Something else entirely?

But right now, none of that mattered. The only thing that mattered was Hannah.

Grabbing his suitcase, Noah hurried out the door of the honeymoon suite, letting it slam shut behind him. He ran down the hallway to the elevator, pressed the button frantically, cursed when it took too long, and then sprinted for the stairs instead.

He had to find her. Had to tell her he loved her. Had to beg for her forgiveness and pray she'd give him another chance.

And after he spoke to Hannah, after he convinced her to stay, to give him one more chance, to believe in them, it would be time to get on the road to Whitefish. Hopefully, she'd be by his side when he arrived. Because he really loved her and wanted to spend the rest of his life with her, even though the thought still terrified him.

But sometimes the best things in life were terrifying. Sometimes you had to be brave enough to take the risk.

Noah just hoped he wasn't too late.

CHAPTER 15

They were due to start boarding in ten minutes, and Hannah was ready. More than ready. She could see the plows clearing the runways through the large windows, their lights flashing as they pushed the snow into massive piles. The sunshine sparkled on the white powder that was piled high along the edges of the tarmac, making everything look pristine and beautiful and completely at odds with the darkness she felt inside.

In Oklahoma, where she'd grown up, it often snowed during the winter months, but nothing like this Montana storm. There must be at least four and a half feet on the ground in some places, drifts even higher where the wind had piled it up. She wondered about the highway conditions and found herself praying, despite everything, that Noah would reach Whitefish safely when he finally left.

Though she was hurt, devastated, really, that he'd made the choice he had, that he'd chosen his fear over their love, she still loved him with every broken piece of her heart. She never wanted harm to come to him. She wanted him to be happy, even if that happiness didn't include her. He would always have a very special place in her heart, a Noah-shaped hole that nothing else would ever fill, but it was time to move on. Time to accept that sometimes love wasn't enough.

With a heavy sigh that seemed to come from the depths of her soul, Hannah picked up her book again and tried desperately to keep her mind occupied, to focus on anything other than the pain radiating through her chest. The words still wouldn't make sense, still swam on the page like they were written in a foreign language.

There was a sudden commotion near the security checkpoint, and Hannah could hear loud voices echoing through the terminal, but she couldn't see anything from where she was sitting. Probably some idiot traveler who didn't understand that you don't argue with TSA agents. They win every single time. It was a losing battle before it even started.

Blocking out the noise, Hannah crawled back into her story, or at least tried to. She read the same sentence seven times without comprehending a single word.

"Hannah," a familiar voice said, breathing heavy and labored.

Her heart stopped. Actually stopped beating for a full second before it kicked back into overdrive.

She glanced up slowly, afraid she was hallucinating, afraid this was just wishful thinking manifesting as auditory hallucinations, to see Noah standing directly in front of her. He was disheveled, his hair sticking up like he'd been running his hands through it, his shirt slightly untucked, his face flushed from exertion. He looked like he'd run a marathon to get here.

"What are you doing here?" Hannah asked, her voice coming out sharper than she'd intended, her defenses immediately snapping into place. "I told you I was going home. I told you we were done."

"I'm an idiot," Noah said without preamble, the words tumbling out in a rush. "A very smart, intelligent doctor who apparently doesn't know the first thing about how to have a relationship with a woman. Especially another doctor who he loves so damn much it terrifies him."

Hannah stared at him, her book forgotten in her lap, her heart pounding so hard she could hear it in her ears. Was he admitting he'd been wrong? He'd just said that he loved her, actually said the words out loud in a crowded airport terminal. Could there be hope? Dare she let herself hope after the devastation of last night?

"When I woke up this morning and realized you were gone, I was completely lost," Noah continued, the words pouring out of him like a confession. "All night, I tossed and turned and couldn't sleep. I kept reaching for you, and you weren't there. I couldn't stop thinking about what I'd said, about how wrong I was, about how I was throwing away the best thing that ever happened to me. I finally fell asleep around five this morning. Then I must have fallen into a coma or something because I never heard you leave. I didn't hear you packing, didn't hear the door close. And when I woke up, you were just... gone."

If he thought that was going to be enough to convince her to stay, to forgive him, he had to think again. Hannah had spent all night and all morning building up her walls, reinforcing her decision, convincing herself that leaving was the right choice. There was only one thing that could stop her from getting on that plane. And it better come with a serious commitment, with a promise of forever, with proof that he was really ready for this.

"My mother was a schizophrenic who often had bouts of losing her grip on reality," Noah said, and Hannah saw the pain flash across his face. "This morning, I called my father and we talked, really talked, for the first time in years about what happened between him and my mother. And I learned things I never knew. It wasn't all him, Hannah. It wasn't even mostly him. It was my mother's illness that caused them to argue the way they did, which made their relationship toxic and unstable. My father was a saint for staying married to her as long as he did, for trying to make it work despite everything."

Hannah felt her anger softening slightly, felt herself leaning forward despite her best efforts to remain distant.

"Two normal doctors who love each other would not argue like my parents did," Noah continued, his eyes locked on hers. "We've never fought like that. We've had disagreements, plenty of them, but you don't scream obscenities at me or throw things or make me feel like I'm worthless. And I don't think you ever would. That's not who you are."

Maybe he should reconsider that assumption, Hannah thought with a flash of dark humor, because last night she'd been ready to yell at him, to shake him, to make him see reason. But she'd realized that screaming would get her nowhere. She'd learned long ago that often the way to be heard the loudest was to speak softly, calmly, with absolute conviction.

"For years, God, for so many years, I've been completely attracted to you," Noah said, taking a step closer. "I've loved you, but was too terrified to take that next step, to risk everything we had for something more. This morning, my father accused me of wanting my cake and eating it too. And he's absolutely right. As long as things went along smoothly between us, as long as I could have you in my life without risking my heart, I didn't have a reason to make any changes to our friendship. I was comfortable. Safe. Cowardly."

Hannah felt tears forming in her eyes, but refused to let them fall. Not yet. Not until she knew where this was going.

"And yet you showed me these last few days how incredible it could be between us," Noah continued, his voice dropping lower, more intimate. "You showed me what I was missing, what I was too afraid to reach for. And I don't want that to end, Hannah. I don't want to lose you. I can't lose you."

In complete disbelief, her breath catching in her throat,

Hannah watched as Noah got down on one knee right there in the middle of the airport terminal. People around them stopped what they were doing, conversations halting mid-sentence as they turned to watch. Noah reached into his jacket pocket and pulled out a small velvet jewelry box.

Speechless, unable to form words even if she'd wanted to, Hannah stared at the ring as he opened the box. A very large emerald-cut diamond shimmered in the fluorescent airport lighting, catching the light and throwing rainbows across Noah's face. It was stunning. Absolutely breathtaking.

"This morning, after I talked to my father, I ran to the jewelry shop the moment they opened for the first time in days," Noah said, his voice shaking slightly. "The owner was just unlocking the door, and I practically knocked him over getting inside. Then I came here and almost got arrested by security because apparently they don't like to let you through the checkpoint when you don't have a ticket. Who knew?"

Despite everything, despite her hurt and her anger and her broken heart, Hannah felt a laugh bubble up in her throat.

"I have maybe five minutes left before that big TSA agent glaring at me from over there comes to physically haul me out of here," Noah said, gesturing behind him where indeed a large, stern-looking TSA agent stood with his arms crossed, watching them with clear disapproval. "So please, Hannah, forgive me. Be patient with me while I learn how to navigate this new direction in our relationship. I've never done this before, never let myself be vulnerable like this, never risked everything for love. But most of all, I'm asking you to love me. Love me and marry me, and spend the rest of our days together. I don't want to lose my best friend. I want my lover by my side for the rest of my life. I want to wake up next to you every morning and fall asleep holding you every night. I want to work beside you and come home to you and build a life with you. I want everything, Hannah. Everything we talked about, everything we dreamed about. I want to give you the world."

Oh my God. Oh my God, he was actually asking her to marry him. This wasn't a dream or a hallucination or wishful thinking. This was real. This was happening.

Warmth spread through Hannah's entire body, starting in her chest and radiating outward until even her fingertips tingled with it. She laughed, a sound of pure joy and disbelief and overwhelming relief as she realized the significance of this moment, as she let herself finally believe it was real.

Dr. Noah Baker was down on one knee in the middle of the Missoula airport, in front of dozens of strangers, asking her to be his wife, to spend forever with him. This moment was what she'd dreamed of for years, literally years, and finally, miraculously, it was coming true.

He gazed at her with such raw fear in those deep sapphire eyes of his, fear that she might say no, that she might reject him the way he'd rejected her. And Hannah knew with absolute certainty that their children would be beautiful, that they would have his eyes and her determination, that they would be so loved it would almost be ridiculous.

Unable to contain herself for another second, Hannah launched herself out of the chair with enough force that it skidded backward. She threw herself at Noah, and they both went down, landing on the airport floor in a tangle of limbs and laughter.

"Yes," Hannah cried, not caring that she was probably shouting, not caring that everyone in the terminal could hear her. "Yes, yes, yes, a thousand times yes! I'll marry you. I love you so damn much, and I never thought you would realize it was me you wanted all along. I thought I'd lost you forever."

"I love you," Noah said, staring into her eyes with such intensity it stole her breath. "I love you more than I thought it was possible to love another person. Sometimes it takes me a while to figure things out, and apparently, you have to knock me over the head before I see what's right in front of me."

Hannah's lips found his before he could say anything else, and while they were lying there on the floor of the Missoula airport terminal with people watching and probably recording them on their phones, Noah kissed her with enough passion that they were definitely making a spectacle of themselves. But Hannah didn't care. Not even a little bit. She'd found her person, her partner, her forever. Everything else was just noise.

His hands came up to cup her face, his thumbs brushing away the tears that were now streaming freely down her cheeks, happy tears this time, tears of joy and relief and overwhelming love.

Finally, they broke apart, both of them breathless and grinning like idiots. Hannah could hear people around them clapping and cheering, could see phones pointed in their direction, but all she could focus on was Noah's face, on the love shining in his eyes.

"Does this mean you'll go to Whitefish with me?" Noah asked, his voice hopeful and slightly uncertain, like he still couldn't quite believe she'd said yes.

"Of course," Hannah said, laughing through her tears. "I need to meet my new mother-in-law. I need to spend Christmas with you and your family. I need to start our life together. I'm not letting you out of my sight ever again."

A big smile spread across Noah's face, the biggest, most genuine smile she'd ever seen from him, and he leaned down and kissed her again, slower this time, sweeter, a promise of everything to come.

A man cleared his throat loudly above them, the sound pointed and impossible to ignore. "You've officially run out of time."

They broke apart reluctantly, and Hannah glanced up to see

the big TSA agent standing over them, looking stern but with the tiniest hint of amusement in his eyes.

Just then, as if perfectly timed for maximum irony, the airline agent at the gate called Hannah's flight number to begin boarding. "Now boarding all rows for Flight 2847 to Denver with continuing service to Houston."

There was no way to get her checked luggage back now, it was probably already loaded on the plane, already on its way to Houston without her. She had packed a smaller carry-on bag for the plane, but it held very few clothes. Just some basic toiletries and a change of underwear. Everything else would be arriving in Houston to an empty apartment.

"I guess my luggage is going back to Houston without me," Hannah said, laughing at the absurdity of it all. "I'm going to show up at your father's house with literally nothing but the clothes on my back and a carry-on bag."

"We'll buy you whatever you need," Noah said, standing up and pulling her to her feet with him. He grabbed her hand, took the ring out of the box with slightly shaking fingers, and slid it onto her left hand. It fit perfectly, like it had been made for her. Like this had always been meant to happen.

"We're officially engaged," Noah said, his voice full of wonder as he stared at the ring on her finger. "No need for us to pretend anymore. This is the real deal, Hannah. Forever and ever. You and me against the world."

The ring was absolutely gorgeous and Hannah gazed down at it in amazement, watching it catch the light, watching it sparkle on her hand. Her hand. Her ring. Her fiancé. The words didn't even seem real yet.

"And you're about to be officially arrested if you don't leave my security area right now," the TSA agent told them, but his voice had softened slightly. "Move it along, lovebirds."

Hannah grinned up at the stern man, feeling giddy and reckless and happier than she'd ever been in her entire life. "How often does everyone in the gate area get to witness a man propose? We gave them a story to tell. That has to count for something."

Shaking his head at the two of them, clearly trying not to smile, the agent pointed firmly to the exit sign. "Out. Now. Before I change my mind about not charging you with trespassing."

Noah grabbed Hannah's carry-on bag in one hand and her hand in the other, and they hurried toward the exit, half-running, both of them laughing like teenagers who'd just pulled off the prank of the century.

Hannah turned back to wave at the TSA agent, who was definitely smiling now despite his best efforts. Then she gazed at the man she loved with all her heart, the man who'd almost let fear destroy them but had found the courage to fight for their love instead.

What a story they would tell their children someday. How their father had almost gotten arrested while proposing to their mother in an airport. How he'd run through security without a ticket because he couldn't let her leave. How he'd gotten down on one knee in front of strangers and declared his love despite his terror. How their mother had tackled him to the floor and said yes without a moment's hesitation.

It was messy and imperfect and absolutely perfect all at once.

Just like them.

"I love you," Hannah said again, because she could say it now, because he wanted to hear it, because she'd never get tired of saying it.

"I love you too," Noah said, pulling her close as they walked through the terminal toward the exit, toward the parking lot, toward Whitefish and Christmas and the beginning of their forever. "I love you so much it terrifies me. But I'm not running anymore. I'm done being afraid."

And as they stepped out into the bright Montana sunshine,

the snow sparkling all around them like diamonds, Hannah knew that everything they'd been through, all the pain and fear and heartbreak, had been worth it to get them to this moment.

This was their beginning.

And it was going to be beautiful.

CHAPTER 16

Four hours later, they pulled into Whitefish, and Noah felt his anxiety ratchet up with every mile they'd gotten closer to this moment. The roads had been treacherous most of the way, ice hidden beneath innocent-looking snow, black ice gleaming in patches where the sun hadn't reached, curves that came up too fast even when you were going slowly. Several times, they had come to a complete stop while emergency vehicles worked to pull someone out of the ditch they'd slid into, their cars crumpled and damaged, reminders of how dangerous these conditions were.

The Jeep had handled the roads like it was made for exactly this kind of terrain, gripping when other vehicles spun out, staying steady when Noah's nerves were anything but. And now, on the edge of town with the familiar landmarks of his father's new home appearing around them, Noah was more nervous than he'd been during his medical boards.

Hannah reached over and squeezed his leg, her touch grounding him the way it always did. "We're almost there. You're going to be fine."

All the way here, during the long, tense drive, they had talked about his parents. Noah had told Hannah everything, things he'd never told anyone before, secrets he'd been carrying since childhood. So much he realized he'd been deeply ashamed of, but now he understood that she needed to know everything if they were going to build a life together. No more secrets. No more walls.

He'd told her about the screaming matches that had echoed through their house late at night, about hiding in his room with his hands over his ears. About the time his mother had thrown a plate at his father, and it had shattered against the wall, leaving a dent in the drywall that had stayed there for years as a reminder. About the medication bottles lined up on the counter, the pills his mother sometimes took and sometimes didn't, depending on whether she believed she needed them.

Including how his mother had committed suicide eight years ago, which had devastated both him and his father in ways they were still processing. She'd walked out on them when Noah was in high school, had severed ties almost completely, but they had never expected her to take her own life. Never imagined she was that far gone. After the divorce, living alone, she'd realized her mental illness had gotten progressively worse, spiraling beyond her control, and she'd ended her life with an overdose of sleeping pills.

Noah had been in his second year of medical school when that happened, studying for an exam on psychiatric disorders of all things, and it had been devastating. The irony hadn't been lost on him, learning about the very illness that had killed his mother while grieving her loss. No matter what had happened between them, no matter how difficult she'd been, he had loved his adoptive mother and accepted that she'd had serious health issues beyond her control.

This Christmas was going to be filled with big, life-changing events. His engagement to Hannah, still so new he kept glancing at the ring on her finger to make sure it was real. Meeting his stepmother for the first time. And whatever other news his father had hinted at, the revelation he'd said needed to happen in person. Noah couldn't help but wonder if his father would finally tell him the truth about his birth mother and father, the story he'd been piecing together from hints and fragments his entire life.

He'd thought about trying to locate them over the years, had even gone so far as to pull up adoption registry websites late at night. But he'd always decided against it, convinced that he loved his parents, the ones who'd raised him, and didn't want to hurt them by seeming ungrateful or curious about the people who'd given him away. Overall, despite everything, despite his mother's illness and the chaos it had created, they had given him a great life. They'd loved him, educated him, supported his dreams.

Since he was a child, maybe five or six years old, Noah had known he was adopted as a baby. His parents had never hidden it from him, had told him in age-appropriate ways that he was chosen, that they'd wanted him desperately. And he'd always wondered what circumstances had led his birth mother to give him up. Had she been too young? Too poor? Had she been forced by her family? Had she wanted to keep him, but couldn't?

When Noah pulled up in front of the house, he was surprised by what he saw. His father had made enough money over his career as a physician that he was considered quite wealthy by most standards, certainly comfortable enough to retire early and live however he wanted. But the house was modest, unassuming, a charming two-story with a wrap-around porch and Christmas lights twinkling in the windows. It looked like a home, not a showpiece.

After parking the Jeep and taking a deep breath to steady himself, Noah came around and helped Hannah out, his hands lingering on her waist. Smiling at her, drinking in her presence like oxygen, he gave her a quick kiss on the lips.

"You drove very well on the ice and snow," Hannah said warmly. "I felt completely safe the entire time."

"Thank you," Noah said, then added carefully, testing the waters, "Any criticism? Any way I could have done better? Any suggestions for the drive back?"

Hannah grinned at him, understanding immediately what he was doing. "None at all. You were perfect. But I'll definitely let you know if I ever have concerns, and I trust you to listen."

The woman was smart and knew exactly what he was trying to show her, that he was willing to listen to her feedback, to her concerns, to her criticisms if they came. That he wasn't going to let them fall back into the defensive trap he had created yesterday. That he'd learned from his catastrophic mistakes. Hopefully, he'd actually learned and wouldn't revert to his old patterns the first time things got difficult.

His father met them at the door before they'd even made it up the porch steps, his face breaking into a huge smile that Noah hadn't seen in years. "You made it! And Hannah is with you. We're so glad. I was worried about the roads."

A tall older woman stood behind his father, her hand resting lightly on his shoulder. She had kind eyes and silver hair pulled back in a elegant twist, and Noah could see genuine warmth in her expression.

"Come in, come in, and meet Wendy," his father said, stepping aside and ushering them into the warm house. The smell of something delicious, cinnamon and apples, wafted from somewhere deeper in the house.

A big smile spread across his father's face, the kind of smile Noah associated with his childhood, before everything had fallen apart. His father wrapped his arm around Wendy's back when they stepped fully into the house, the gesture casual and affectionate and so different from the way he'd moved around Noah's mother.

"Noah and Hannah, this is Wendy," his father said, his voice full of pride and happiness.

Noah held out his hand formally, but Wendy ignored it

completely and pulled him into a warm hug instead. "I'm so glad you're finally here. Your father has been talking about you nonstop for weeks. Welcome to our home."

There was a warmth about her, an openness and genuine kindness, that Noah had never experienced with his adoptive mother. His mother had been brilliant but cold, loving but distant, affectionate on her terms but never on his. This woman radiated acceptance and warmth.

Pulling back from the hug, Noah stared at her and then at his father, seeing the way they looked at each other with such obvious affection. They both had big smiles and contentment radiating from them, and Noah would bet everything he owned that they would be together until the very end, that they'd found something rare and precious.

"Thank you," Noah said, his voice thick with emotion he hadn't expected. "I can tell my father is very happy with you, and that's wonderful to see. I haven't seen him like this in... I can't remember how long."

Wendy grinned, her entire face lighting up, and then she took Noah by one arm and Hannah by the other, linking them together like they were all old friends. "Come on in, there is so much to talk about. And I see there is a beautiful ring on Hannah's finger that wasn't there when your father described you two. I'm so happy for you both."

Astonished by this woman's perceptiveness and genuine enthusiasm, Noah walked with her into the big family room. The space was decorated for Christmas, a tree in the corner covered in ornaments that looked handmade, stockings hanging from the mantle, and garland wrapped around the staircase railing.

"She said yes," Noah announced, unable to keep the pride and wonder out of his voice. "At the airport this morning. I almost got arrested, but she said yes."

"Good," his father said, laughing. "Hannah, I've been waiting for years for this day. I've been telling Noah for at least three years that you two were perfect for each other."

"Me too," Hannah said, laughing along with him. "It took him long enough to realize that I was the one. I was starting to think I'd have to hit him over the head with something heavy."

"He's a very smart man when it comes to medicine," his father said with affectionate exasperation, "but he's a little slow and overly cautious when it comes to commitment. And I blame myself and Francis for that. We showed him the worst possible example of what a marriage could be."

They settled onto the comfortable couches, and Noah could see that his father was nervous, his hands fidgeting slightly, his smile not quite reaching his eyes despite his obvious happiness. Something was coming. Something big.

"Do you like living back here?" Hannah asked his father, bless her for making small talk when Noah couldn't seem to form words. "It's so different from Houston. I imagine it must have been quite an adjustment."

His father gave a warm chuckle. "Yes, it's completely different. But you see, Wendy was here. We went to high school together right here in Whitefish. We dated back then, were quite serious, actually, but we were young and stupid and broke up when we both went off to different colleges. Life took us in different directions. I went to medical school, got married, had a career. She got married, had children, built a life. But not long ago, after I retired and moved back, we found each other again at a high school reunion of all places. And here we are. Second chances."

Wendy reached out and took his father's hand, squeezing it gently. "My husband had passed away two years earlier, and of course, your mother had passed as well. We were both starting over, both looking for something we didn't even know we needed."

"What a wonderful story," Hannah said sincerely. "I'm so

happy for you both. You can see how much you care for each other. Do you have children, Wendy?"

"Yes, three," Wendy said, her face lighting up. "Two daughters and a son. But they're not going to arrive until the day after Christmas, they have commitments with their in-laws for Christmas Day. We can't wait for all of you to meet, but in the meantime, we're going to have dinner at the Miller's house tomorrow night. Christmas Eve dinner."

His stepmother gave a pointed look at his father, and Noah could see that she was prompting him, encouraging him to say whatever it was he'd been working up to.

Noah's stomach tightened with anticipation and dread. "What's going on, Dad? You said on the phone that you had something important to tell me. Something that couldn't wait but needed to be said in person."

His father took a deep breath, glancing at Wendy for support before turning back to Noah. "When I returned to Whitefish last year, I ran into your birth mother. Beth Miller. We've stayed in touch over the years, Christmas cards, the occasional phone call. She still lives here, has lived here your entire life. And she wants to meet you, Noah. She's wanted to meet you for years but didn't know if you'd want to meet her."

Startled, feeling like the floor had dropped out from under him, Noah had no idea his birth mother lived here in Whitefish. All this time, she'd been here. He suddenly remembered his adoptive mother had always sworn that she never wanted to go to Whitefish, that she never wanted to visit even though it was his father's hometown. Could this be the reason why? Had she known? Had she been afraid?

"I didn't know she lived here," Noah said, his voice sounding strange to his own ears. "You never told me anything about her except that she was young when I was born."

"Yes, she still lives here, in the same house she grew up in, actually," his father said carefully. "But I want to wait and let her tell you the story of how you came into this world, why she made the decisions she made. I feel like it's her story to tell you, not mine. She deserves that."

Stupefied, Noah sat there trying to process this information. His birth mother. Here. Wanting to meet him after thirty-three years. "But you're my father," he said, needing to make that clear, needing his dad to understand. "And though my adoptive mother had serious issues, though things were difficult, I still loved her. I still love you both. Meeting my birth mother doesn't change that."

"Of course it doesn't, sweetheart," Wendy said gently, and Noah appreciated her steady presence. "She was the mother you knew, the mother who raised you. No one is trying to replace that or diminish it."

"Yes, exactly," his father said, emotion thick in his voice. "And while I may have had no biological hand in creating you, Francis and I loved you more than anything in this world. You saved us in a lot of ways. After she was diagnosed with schizophrenia shortly after we married, we made the difficult decision not to have children naturally. We didn't want to risk passing on her condition. But we desperately wanted to be parents. Then, when I learned through... through connections here... that you were going to be put up for adoption, we contacted the family and made the arrangements. It seemed like fate."

Hannah reached out and touched Noah on the arm, her presence anchoring him. "Are you okay with this? Meeting her? Because you don't have to if you're not ready."

How often did adoptees get this opportunity? So many people spent their entire lives wondering, searching, hoping for answers that never came. And here Noah was, being handed his history on a silver platter. The story of where he came from, who he was, why he'd been given up.

"Are you okay with this, Dad?" Noah asked, searching his father's face. "My feelings will never change for you. You're my father in every way that matters. But I'd be lying if I said I wasn't curious."

The man grinned, his eyes shining with unshed tears. "Yes, son. I think it's time you learned the truth, but I want Beth to tell you herself. It's her story and yours, and she's been carrying it alone for over thirty years. She deserves to share it with you."

Beth. His birth mother's name was Beth and he was going to meet her tomorrow. The knowledge felt surreal, like something happening to someone else.

"When are we meeting them?" Noah asked, his hand finding Hannah's and gripping it tightly. "You said them. Is there... is my birth father going to be there too?"

His father exchanged a meaningful look with Wendy. "Tomorrow, Christmas Eve. We thought tonight we'd spend time together as a family, just the four of us. Let you settle in, process this news. Then tomorrow, Beth and her family want us to come to dinner at their house. And yes, your birth father will be there. They never married, but they've remained... close. You'll understand more when you meet them."

Hannah took his hand with both of hers now and squeezed it, her touch saying everything words couldn't. "This is turning out to be quite the Christmas."

Noah grinned at her despite his churning emotions, despite the anxiety and anticipation and fear coursing through him. "Yes, yes, it is. Quite the Christmas indeed."

He was getting married to the love of his life. He'd met a stepmother who seemed genuinely wonderful. And tomorrow, on Christmas Eve, he was going to meet the woman who'd given birth to him and given him up, the woman who'd made the hardest decision a mother could make.

His life was changing in ways he couldn't have imagined just days ago.

And for the first time in a very long time, Noah felt like maybe—just maybe—all the pieces were finally falling into place.

CHAPTER 17

The next day, his father, Wendy, Hannah, and Noah drove to a house less than a mile from his father's place. With a swirl of emotion going through him, anticipation, anxiety, hope, fear, Noah stared at the modest two-story house where his birth mother lived. Where she'd lived his entire life, just a mile from where his father had grown up. All these years, she'd been right here.

"Oh, by the way," his father said casually, though Noah could hear the slight tension in his voice, "she has three daughters. You have three half-sisters."

Noah felt his breath catch. He'd never thought about having siblings, had grown up as an only child, had imagined he'd always be an only child. And now, at thirty-three years old, he was about to meet three sisters he never knew existed. Warmth filled him at the thought, spreading through his chest like sunshine. Yet immediately following that warmth came uncertainty. How would they feel when they learned they had a brother? Would they resent him? Would they see him as an intruder in their family?

When they reached the door, before Noah's father could even knock, a woman stepped outside. She was in her early fifties, with striking features and eyes that immediately drew Noah's attention. Her eyes were filling with tears as she looked at him, really looked at him, drinking in every detail of his face.

"Noah?" she asked, her voice trembling.

"Yes," Noah said, grinning at her despite his nerves, despite the emotion threatening to overwhelm him. "I'm Noah."

He had her eyes. The realization hit him like a physical blow. He had her beautiful blue eyes, the exact same shade, the same shape. And her mouth and nose too. The resemblance was unmistakable. But her hair was a vibrant red, going gray at the temples, while he had inherited dark hair from somewhere else. From his father, he assumed.

"Oh my God," Beth breathed, and then she threw her arms around him without hesitation, without asking permission. A sob escaped her throat, raw and painful and full of thirty-three years of grief and longing. "You have to know I never wanted to give you up. Not for a single moment. I've thought of you every day since the moment we were separated. Every birthday, every Christmas, every milestone, I wondered where you were, what you were doing, if you were happy."

It felt surprisingly natural to wrap his arms around her, this stranger who was also his mother, and Noah held on tightly. She smelled nice, something floral and warm, and he couldn't help but think: this is my mother. Not the woman who raised me, not the woman I called Mom growing up, but the woman who gave birth to me, who carried me for nine months, who made an impossible choice.

"Please don't hate me," Beth said against his shoulder, her voice muffled and desperate. "Please tell me you don't hate me for giving you away."

"How could I hate you?" Noah said, surprised by the conviction in his own voice, by how much he meant it. "I've had a wonderful life. Two parents who loved me, a good education, and opportunities I might never have had otherwise. And now I'm getting to meet you. But I will admit, I'm very curious about why you gave me up, and who my father is—was."

Beth sniffed and leaned back in his arms, studying his face with wonder, like she was trying to memorize every feature. "Come in and meet the others. They don't know about you yet. I want you all to hear the story at the same time, together as a family. Charles knows this tale, but he graciously wanted me to be the one to tell you."

"Beth," Noah's father said gently, his own eyes shining with unshed tears, "I've had Noah for all these years. Thirty-three years of watching him grow up, of being his father. It's time you got to know him and for him to know the truth about you and his real father."

"Thank you, Charles," Beth said, sniffing and wiping at her eyes. "Thank you for raising him so well. Thank you for bringing him back to me." She turned her attention to Hannah, seeming to notice her for the first time. "And who is this beautiful young woman?"

"This is my fiancée Hannah," Noah said, unable to keep the pride from his voice as he pulled Hannah close. "Dr. Hannah Young. We just got engaged yesterday."

Beth grasped Hannah's hand in both of hers, her grip warm and strong. "So nice to meet you, dear. This blizzard has brought so many of us together, hasn't it? Reunited so many people. Now come on in, all of you. Everyone is here and they're going to be so surprised. I haven't told them anything, I wanted this to be a moment we all share."

When they stepped inside the door, a tall, distinguished-looking man with silver hair stood from where he'd been sitting. "This is my husband John," Beth said, her voice steadier now. "John, this is Noah."

Inside the large family room, the fireplace was blazing cheerfully, casting dancing shadows on the walls. A large Christmas tree stood in the corner, covered in ornaments that looked collected over years, handmade ones, photo ornaments, special keepsakes. But the main thing that caught Noah's eye was the three women sitting around the room in various chairs and on the couch. His sisters. He had sisters. The knowledge felt surreal, impossible, wonderful.

His birth mother took her husband's hand, Noah noticed how naturally they moved together, how comfortable they were, and they walked into the center of the room together, facing everyone.

"Have a seat, Noah and Hannah," Beth said, gesturing to an empty loveseat. "Charles and Wendy, please sit as well."

They sank down on the loveseat, Hannah's hand finding Noah's immediately, anchoring him. The three girls were staring at one another, exchanging confused glances, clearly wondering what was going on. Noah could see the looks they gave each other, silent sister communication that spoke volumes. They had no idea who he was or why their mother had asked them all to be here. Boy, were they in for a shock.

His birth mother glanced at her husband, who nodded encouragingly, and then she took a deep breath that Noah could hear from across the room. "The reason I wanted all of you to come for Christmas, insisted that you all be here, is to meet Noah and his fiancée, Hannah. You're probably wondering who he is and why this is so important." She paused, gathering her courage. "Well, he's your brother. Your older brother."

The girls all gasped in unison. One of them, heavily pregnant, her belly enormous, looked like she might faint. In fact, it appeared the baby could arrive at any moment.

"What?" the pregnant woman said, her hand going protectively to her belly. "When did you have him? How is this possible?"

"He's our brother," a dark-haired girl said, her voice full of wonder rather than accusation. She jumped up from her chair and ran across the room to Noah, pulling him into an enthusiastic hug before he could even stand. "I'm Olivia. I've always wanted a brother. Especially someone older than me who can take some of the heat off. Now you can deal with the golden girls and their drama."

Golden girls? Noah had no idea what she was talking about, but he hugged her back, charmed by her immediate acceptance. He noticed the other two girls were identical twins, both blonde, both beautiful, both staring at him with a mixture of shock and curiosity.

The first blonde rose gracefully and came over, giving him a warm hug. "I'm one of the so-called golden girls, Emily. But I'm not the one she's really referring to. Even nine months pregnant and ready to pop, Amelia always manages to get all the attention." She turned and sat in a chair next to a very distinguished-looking man, whom Noah assumed was her husband.

"I'm Amelia," the pregnant girl said, not attempting to get up from where she was deeply embedded in an armchair. "Excuse me if I don't get up, I haven't been able to stand without assistance for two weeks. And I'm the one they lovingly refer to as the golden girl because I'm the overachiever of the family. Straight A's, perfect attendance, early acceptance to law school. I'm also apparently the only one who could get pregnant while using a condom correctly."

Noah laughed, not entirely certain if she was being serious or sarcastic. There seemed to be some playful tension in the room, the kind of ribbing that came from siblings who loved each other but also drove each other crazy. He wondered about the family dynamics, about how they would truly feel about him once the shock wore off. Would they be welcoming of him as their brother in the long run?

"Now that you've all met," Beth said, glancing around the room at her children, all four of them, "I want to tell you the story of how Noah came into this world."

Her husband put his hand on her back supportively, and she sighed deeply, preparing herself for what Noah could tell was going to be a difficult story.

"When I was sixteen years old," Beth began, her voice steady but thick with emotion, "I fell madly, desperately in love with a young man. The kind of first love that feels like it will last forever. We were high school sweethearts, and we planned our entire life together. We talked about where we'd go to college, how many kids we'd have, and where we'd live. He even gave me a promise ring. I wore it every single day."

Her daughters were all staring at her with rapt attention, their husbands, Noah assumed they were their husbands, sitting quietly beside them. No one had really explained who these men were, but their presence suggested commitment, family.

"Greg Baker was his name," Beth said, and Noah felt his heart skip a beat. Baker, the same last name as his adoptive father. "And we vowed that no one would ever come between us. We were naïve and young and so certain of our love." She paused, tears forming. "No one ever did come between us. But fate had other plans."

Beth turned her attention specifically to Noah, her eyes locking with his. "You have the same facial structure as your father. The same height and hair coloring. The same way of tilting your head when you're thinking. You remind me so much of him, Noah. I have several pictures I saved for you, hoping against hope that I'd meet you someday and be able to show you the man who was your father."

"Thank you," Noah said, his throat tight with emotion. "But what happened? Why did you give me up for adoption? What happened to my father?"

Beth took a shuddering breath. "It was high school graduation night. I was already suspicious that I was pregnant, my period was late, I was feeling sick in the mornings, but I hadn't told him yet. I was certain we would get married that summer like we'd planned, and then go on to college together with our baby. Little did I know about how much time and energy babies require, how much our lives would have changed."

With a sigh that seemed to come from the depths of her soul, Beth glanced around the room, making sure she had everyone's attention. "The night of graduation, we celebrated with some friends at a bonfire. There was no drinking at this party; we just danced, laughed, and enjoyed being young and alive and finally done with high school. Greg took me home around eleven-thirty and kissed me goodnight. He promised he would call and let me know he'd gotten home safely. It was something we always did, called to say we'd made it home."

She wiped a tear away with the back of her hand. "It was after midnight, and he didn't call. I called him, but no one answered. I told myself he'd fallen asleep, that he'd call in the morning. But I couldn't sleep. Something felt wrong."

The room had gone completely silent. Even the fire seemed to quiet.

"The next morning, I went to his house and found police cars in the driveway. I learned that he was killed by a drunk driver that night on his way home from my house. The driver ran a red light and hit Greg's car on the driver's side. He died instantly. All the dreams we'd shared of getting married and going to school together and growing old together died that night on a stretch of road less than two miles from my house."

Her husband patted her on the back as she struggled to compose herself. Her daughters were crying openly now.

"That's why you never would let us stay out after midnight," Olivia said, understanding dawning. "Why you went into a panic if we were even five minutes late?"

"Why you didn't like us on the road late at night," Emily added.

"Why you warned us constantly about drinking and driving," Amelia finished. "We thought you were being overprotective. We had no idea."

"Yes," Beth said simply. "I couldn't lose a child to a late-night accident. I couldn't survive it."

She took a moment to collect herself before continuing. "A month after Greg's funeral, I knew for certain I was pregnant. I was seventeen years old, alone, and carrying the baby of the boy I'd loved and lost. Part of me was thrilled. I still had a piece of Greg, still had something of him in this world. And yet I knew my parents would not be happy. I had no idea how unhappy they would be."

A pained expression crossed her face, and Noah had the overwhelming urge to get up and go to her, to comfort her somehow. He couldn't imagine being in her predicament, seventeen, alone, grieving, pregnant.

"My parents packed me up and sent me to a maternity home three states away. They told everyone I was going to stay with an aunt who was sick. No one knew the truth. I spent six months in that home with other girls in my situation, all of us waiting to give birth, all of us knowing we'd have to give our babies away."

"When Noah was born," Beth continued, her voice breaking, "I was told a family had already been chosen for him. My parents made it abundantly clear that I had no choice but to accept the adoption. I had no education beyond high school, no money, no job, nothing. And they would not help me raise him. They said I'd made my choice by getting pregnant, and now I had to face the consequences. I've never felt so alone, so helpless, so distraught in my life. Here was the baby of the man that I had loved and lost, and they were forcing me to give him up. I held him for one hour after he was born, memorized every detail of his face, and then they took him away."

Noah couldn't help himself, he rose from the loveseat and went to Beth, wrapping his arms around her. What an impossible choice she'd had to make. What grief she must have carried all these years.

"What I didn't know at the time," Beth said, sobbing against Noah's shoulder, "was that Greg's cousin Charles and his wife Francis were adopting you. It wasn't until years later that I learned the truth. By then, your mother, Francis, had made it clear she didn't want me in your life. And I understood. I didn't want to disrupt your world. But I never stopped thinking about you. Never stopped wondering. Never stopped hoping that someday, somehow, I'd get to meet you."

Beth held onto him tightly, and Noah held her right back, this woman who'd given him life and given him away and never forgotten him.

"After I was forced to give you up," she continued, her voice muffled against his shoulder, "I made the decision that I would do everything I could to always be independent and able to take care of myself. I went to college, got a degree, and started a career. I married John, and we had three beautiful daughters. No one would ever take anything away from me again. I took control of my life. And now look, thirty-three years later, Noah is back in my life, and I couldn't be happier. My son came home for Christmas."

The three girls all rose as one and came over to their mother, and the five of them formed a group hug, Noah and his birth mother surrounded by his three sisters he'd just met.

"We're going to make this the best Christmas ever," Olivia said fiercely. "We're all together now. All of us."

"And Noah, welcome to the family," John said, standing and extending his hand. "I've known about you for years, but didn't know how to locate you. Beth tried to find you several times over the years, but the adoption records were sealed. I'm so glad we finally found you. Or rather, that you found us."

Noah had to wipe the tears away from his eyes. He had a whole new family, three sisters, a brother-in-law soon to be uncle to a niece or nephew, a birth mother who'd never forgotten him, and a stepfather who welcomed him. And his father had remarried Wendy, and they seemed absolutely perfect for one another. Plus, he was engaged to Hannah, the love of his life. Everything had happened at once, and it felt overwhelming and right and perfect all at the same time.

So many questions he'd had about why he'd been given up for adoption were finally answered, and for the first time that he could remember, Noah felt at peace about his background. Now he knew why he'd been adopted. Now he knew about his mother and even something about his father. Now the missing pieces of his identity had been filled in.

But more than anything, Noah felt surrounded by a sense of belonging and happiness he couldn't remember ever experiencing. He was loved by so many people in so many ways.

"Oh," Amelia cried suddenly, her hand flying to her enormous belly. "This baby is playing soccer. I swear she's trying out for the Olympic women's team. That was a hard kick."

The moment of tension broke, and everyone laughed.

"I'm so sorry you had to go through all of that," Noah said to Beth, cupping her face in his hands. "But I want you to know that I was very loved and taken care of. Francis had her struggles, but she loved me. And Dad was—is—amazing. But it means so much to know the story of where I came from, why the choices were made. Thank you for telling me. Thank you for never forgetting me."

Beth hugged him tightly. "Son, I'm so glad I ran into your father here in town last year. I'm so glad that he and Francis adopted you and raised you to be the man you are. You've become a good man, a doctor who helps people, and I'm so proud of you. So incredibly proud."

Warmth filled Noah, and he glanced across the room at his

father, Charles, who was wiping away his own tears. Even Hannah was softly crying, her hands pressed to her mouth.

This was family. This was love. This was where he came from and where he was going.

And it was more than he'd ever dreamed possible.

CHAPTER 18

$\mathcal{C}$hristmas Day dawned bright and beautiful, the sun streaming through the windows and casting golden light across the snow-covered landscape of Whitefish. Noah sat in Beth's cozy kitchen, drinking coffee with his birth mother and Hannah, feeling more content than he could ever remember feeling in his entire life. They had come over early Christmas morning, too excited to sleep in, too eager to spend every possible moment together, and his father and Wendy were going to join them later to have lunch. A real family Christmas dinner with everyone together.

He had gotten to know his sisters a little more over the past twenty-four hours, and Noah genuinely liked them all. Even Amelia, the self-proclaimed golden child, was competitive and driven and apparently capable of getting pregnant despite proper contraceptive use. Each sister had her own distinct personality, Olivia's enthusiasm and warmth, Emily's grace and quiet strength, and Amelia's sharp wit and intelligence. But more than anything, Noah treasured the sense of family and unconditional love that radiated throughout this house. It was so different from the home he'd grown up in, where tension had always simmered beneath the surface, where you never quite knew what mood his mother would be in.

"This is your father's high school picture," Beth said, interrupting his thoughts as she handed him a worn photograph with slightly bent corners, clearly handled many times over the years.

Noah stared into a face that looked remarkably like his own, the same strong jawline, the same deep-set eyes, the same slight crook to the smile. It was like looking into a mirror that reflected back thirty-three years into the past. The young man in the photo looked happy, confident, and ready to take on the world. He had no idea his life would end in just a few short months.

"You should go by and meet his parents, your grandparents," Beth said softly, watching Noah's face as he studied the photo. "I'll even go with you if you want. I think they're still alive, they'd be in their seventies now. They would be absolutely overjoyed to meet you. They were so angry with me for the longest time because I'd given you away, but I had no choice. I tried to explain, but they were grieving their son and couldn't see past their own pain. Maybe now, all these years later, meeting you would bring them some peace."

Picking up the photo, Noah turned it over and glanced at the writing on the back in faded blue ink: *Greg Baker, High School Graduation, June 1991.* He sighed, feeling the weight of history, of tragedy, of time lost that could never be recovered.

Hannah leaned over and looked at the picture in his hands, then up at Noah's face. "I see the resemblance. It's remarkable, actually. The eyes, especially."

His birth mother had several other pictures of Greg spread out on the kitchen table, photos from football games, prom, casual snapshots with friends. Then Beth picked up one particular photo and gave a little sob, her hand trembling slightly. "This one was taken the night he died. The night of graduation."

It was a photo of the two of them in their caps and gowns, arms wrapped around each other, both grinning at the camera with pure joy. They were so young, impossibly young to Noah's eyes now, so eager, so thrilled to be starting the next part of their lives together. So full of hope and dreams and plans for their future. And yet tragically, horrifically, Greg had died just hours after this photo was taken, never knowing that Beth was carrying his child.

Noah felt tears prick his eyes as he stared at the photo. This young man was his father. This laughing boy had loved Beth and died too soon and never got to meet his son. Never got to hold him, teach him to throw a baseball, help him with homework, or watch him graduate from medical school.

Before Noah could say anything, before he could process the emotion welling up inside him, Ryan, Amelia's soon to be husband, came running into the kitchen, his face flushed with panic and excitement.

"Amelia's in labor," he announced breathlessly, running his hands through his hair. "She didn't tell me, classic Amelia move, but she's apparently had contractions since early this morning. We're less than a minute apart now. I'm not certain we have time to get to the hospital. I think she's going to have this baby right here, right now."

From the tone of his voice and the wild look in his eyes, Noah could tell Ryan was worried but also thrilled. This was about to be a father, and the reality of it was hitting him all at once.

"Let me examine her," Hannah said immediately, her doctor instincts kicking in as she rose from her chair with the grace and confidence Noah had always admired. She went to the sink and scrubbed her hands thoroughly, all the way up to her elbows, while Ryan paced nervously. Then she followed him into the bedroom where Amelia walked the floor.

Five minutes later, five minutes that felt like an eternity to Noah, Hannah came rushing back into the kitchen, her eyes bright with excitement and urgency.

"Noah, I need you. Now," Hannah said, already moving back

toward the bedroom. "We're going to help Ryan deliver his baby. She's fully dilated and the baby's coming whether we're ready or not."

They all jumped up at once, Beth, Olivia, Emily, and Noah. Noah went to the sink and scrubbed his hands the way he'd done thousands of times before surgeries and procedures, but this felt different. This was his sister. His niece or nephew. His family.

Following Hannah, Noah stepped into the bedroom to see Ryan positioned at Amelia's feet. He'd placed several clean towels beneath her, and Amelia was breathing heavily, her face flushed and sweaty, her hands gripping the bedsheets.

"You're doing great, honey," Ryan said, his voice shaking slightly. "Though I have to say, on our second child, would you please tell me when you're actually in labor instead of insisting you just have indigestion?"

"Who said there's going to be a second one?" Amelia panted, glaring at him between contractions. "If I live through this, there won't be any more children. I'm done. We're getting you neutered."

Her parents and sisters were standing right outside the door, trying to see in, offering encouragement and support.

"Here it comes," Amelia cried suddenly, starting to pant rapidly the way they'd taught her in birthing classes. "Oh God, it's happening."

"You're doing so good," Hannah said, moving to Amelia's side and lifting her shoulders slightly. "When the next contraction comes, I need you to press down as hard as you can. Noah, get ready to support Ryan if he needs help."

Ryan knelt between Amelia's legs, and Noah knew better than to try to take over. This was Ryan's daughter, and he wanted, needed, to deliver her himself. Noah would only step in if there was an emergency, if something went wrong. But he'd be right here, ready to help if needed.

Amelia screamed, a primal sound of effort and pain and determination.

"The baby's head is crowning," Ryan said, his voice filled with wonder and excitement. "I can see her! She's almost here. Come on, honey, you're doing so great. One more big push."

It was Christmas Day, and Noah couldn't think of a better gift than witnessing new life entering the world. He glanced up at Hannah, who was coaching Amelia through her breathing, and saw tears streaming down Hannah's face. His heart swelled with love and longing. He wanted this with her. He wanted them to have children together, to create life, to raise babies who would know they were loved and wanted. He wanted his children to know their background and where they came from, to have answers to the questions that had haunted Noah for so long. He wanted them to be part of this extended family, to have cousins and grandparents and aunts and uncles who would love them.

"One more big push," Ryan repeated, his hands steady despite his obvious emotion. "You can do this, Amelia."

Amelia cursed loudly, words Noah had never heard his sister say, and screamed just as the infant's head popped out, dark hair already visible. Ryan carefully cleared the mucus from the baby's mouth and nose with practiced movements, then supported the shoulders as he gently guided them out, and suddenly the baby slipped into his waiting hands.

"Welcome to the world, little one," Ryan said, tears streaming down his cheeks, his voice breaking with emotion. "Welcome to our family."

The baby let out a strong, healthy wail that filled the room and brought tears to everyone's eyes.

"Give her to me," Amelia said, crying and laughing at the same time, reaching for her daughter. "I want to meet my daughter. I want to hold her."

Ryan laid the baby carefully on Amelia's stomach, and Noah

watched his sister's face transform with pure love and wonder as she looked at her child for the first time.

"She's so pretty," Amelia whispered, touching the baby's tiny fingers, counting her toes. "She's perfect. Look at all that dark hair."

The baby had a full head of dark hair that stuck up in all directions, and long lashes lay on her cheeks as she kept trying to open her eyes and look around at this strange new world she'd entered.

Amelia took a deep breath, and then her expression changed, a look of confusion and pain crossing her face. Noah's doctor instincts went on high alert. They needed to deliver the afterbirth, but something seemed off.

"It hurts," Amelia said, breathing hard again. "It feels like another contraction. Is that normal? It shouldn't hurt this much, should it?"

Rushing to her side, Noah put his hands on her stomach, palpating carefully. His eyes widened as he felt what he suspected. "I don't think you're done, Amelia. I think you're having twins."

She gasped, her eyes going wide with shock. "But the sonogram didn't show twins. We had multiple ultrasounds. They never saw two babies."

Hannah gave a knowing chuckle, the kind of laugh that comes from years of working in delivery rooms. "One of them was hiding. It happens more often than you'd think, one baby tucked behind the other, hiding from the ultrasound."

"Mom," Noah yelled toward the door, raising his voice so Beth could hear him. "Call an ambulance. We need one here now."

"They're already on their way," Beth replied immediately. "I called as soon as Hannah said Amelia was in active labor."

"Is something wrong?" Amelia asked, fear creeping into her voice as she held her newborn daughter protectively. "Is the baby okay?"

"No, nothing's wrong," Noah reassured her quickly. "But we're not going to take any chances. If you're having twins, the second baby might be smaller, might need additional support. We need to get both babies to the hospital anyway and get them checked out properly, make sure everything is good. Now, do you think you can do this again?"

A tear slipped down Amelia's cheek, but she nodded with determination. "I'll do my best. I'm an overachiever, remember? If I'm going to have babies, apparently I have to have two at once."

Hannah picked up the newborn carefully from Amelia's stomach and wrapped her snugly in a soft blanket. "You've got this. You already did it once, you can do it again."

"Damn overachiever," Olivia said from out in the hallway in a laughing manner, but Noah could tell she didn't say it to be mean. It was said with affection, with pride, with the kind of teasing that only siblings who truly loved each other could get away with. "Of course she's having twins. One baby wasn't enough of an accomplishment."

"Come on, you can do this," Hannah encouraged as she handed the infant to Beth, who cradled her new granddaughter with tears streaming down her face.

A big contraction hit Amelia and she moaned, her body tensing. "Why two, Ryan? Why couldn't we have just one like normal people?"

"Honey, we talked about wanting multiple children," Ryan said, stroking her hair. "This way we get it all done at once. I'm thrilled. But I do hope this one is a boy, give our daughter a brother to watch out for her."

"Easy for you to say," Amelia panted. "You're not the one pushing them out."

Ten minutes later, ten minutes of coaching and breathing and encouragement, Amelia screamed and pressed down once again with all her remaining strength.

"I see the crown," Ryan said, his voice filled with renewed

excitement. "Come on, honey, you're doing amazing. You're going to be the best mom. Just one more push."

"Easy for you to say, you haven't pushed two bowling balls out of your vagina," Amelia said, breathing heavily, sweat pouring down her face.

"Come on, one more big push," Ryan cried, his hands ready to catch their second child.

Noah watched with wonder as his sister gave birth again, this time to a baby boy who came out screaming at the top of his tiny lungs. He was not happy about having to leave that warm, safe cocoon where he'd been comfortable. His face was red and scrunched up with indignation.

"A little boy," Ryan whispered in awe, holding his son for the first time. "We have a son."

Noah cut the umbilical cord, and the baby screamed even louder as he lost his physical connection with his mother.

Noah moved Ryan gently out of the way. "You delivered both babies, you did an amazing job. Now let me take care of the afterbirth and make sure everything else is okay. Go be with your wife and your babies."

Ryan nodded gratefully, too overcome with emotion to speak. He carried his newborn son over to Amelia, who now had both babies in her arms, one on each side.

Noah nodded to Hannah and the two of them worked together seamlessly, the way they always did. They massaged Amelia's stomach to help deliver the afterbirth, and in a matter of minutes, Noah had successfully delivered it and confirmed that everything looked healthy. Hannah cleaned Amelia up, removed the soiled towels, and placed fresh, clean ones beneath her.

Then they opened the door for the family to see the babies. Beth had been inside the room the entire time, but now John, Olivia, and Emily crowded in, everyone wanting to meet the newest members of the family.

Beth was holding baby number one, the little girl, rocking her gently and whispering to her. Ryan was holding tightly to baby number two, the boy, looking like he might never let go.

Noah and Hannah stepped out of the bedroom, giving the new family some space, and Noah pulled Hannah into his arms in the hallway.

"Good job, Doctor," Hannah said, smiling up at him.

"I want what they have," Noah said, gazing into her eyes, meaning every word. "Seeing those babies being born made me want to have children more than I ever have before. Babies with you. A whole houseful of them."

Hannah grinned up at him and kissed him softly on the lips. "Me too. Let's get married and start working on that right away."

The doorbell rang, interrupting their moment, and Hannah hurried to let the paramedics in.

Noah could hear her voice from the front of the house, cheerful and excited, and his heart melted with love for this woman who was going to be his wife.

"Merry Christmas," Hannah said to the paramedics. "We just delivered twins. Surprise twins!"

"Twins?" The men laughed in disbelief. "Well, that's a Christmas miracle. Where's the lucky mother?"

They followed Hannah down the hall, and Noah stepped aside to let them through to the bedroom.

"Are you ready to go to the hospital?" one of the paramedics asked Amelia professionally.

Amelia smiled at them, exhausted but radiant. "Give me just a moment. I need to say something to my family first."

She glanced around the room at everyone gathered there, her husband, her parents, her sisters, and Noah.

"Thank you, Noah and Hannah, for helping Ryan bring our babies into the world," Amelia said, her voice thick with emotion. "It means so much to us. I'm so glad you're a part of our family now. And Olivia and Emily, I'm so glad you're my sisters. We just started a new generation, the next chapter of our family. These babies are going to need cousins to play with and get into trouble with. So you two need to get started on that."

They all hugged and laughed, and Noah couldn't remember a happier Christmas in his entire life. This was what family was supposed to feel like, joy and love and support and laughter, even in the midst of chaos.

As the paramedics loaded Amelia carefully onto the stretcher, they placed one baby in her arm and the other in Ryan's. The little family looked complete, perfect, exactly as it was meant to be.

"We'll meet you at the hospital," Noah said as he watched them wheel his sister out, along with his brand-new niece and nephew. "Drive safely."

His mother, Beth, stood in the hall crying happy tears. Noah wrapped his arms around her, and she held onto him tightly.

"Merry Christmas, Mom," Noah said, the word feeling both strange and right on his tongue. "This has been the best Christmas ever. Thank you for letting me be part of your family."

She hugged him even tighter. "Thank you, son. Thank you for being here, for helping Amelia, for coming back into my life. I prayed for this day for thirty-three years. And thank you for bringing Hannah. I'm so glad you and Hannah were here for this. Now let's get going, we need to be at the hospital with Amelia."

A grin spread across Noah's face, and he turned to gaze at Hannah, who was gathering her coat and purse, chatting with Olivia about the babies.

"Soon," Noah said, pulling Hannah close. "Let's have a baby soon. Let's get married and start our own family."

Hannah blew him a kiss, her eyes shining with love and promise. "I love you, Noah Baker. I love you so much."

"I love you," Noah said, taking her hand and lacing their fingers together as they walked toward the door.

Outside, the snow was still pristine and white, sparkling in the Christmas morning sun. His father and Wendy were just pulling into the driveway, waving excitedly when they saw everyone rushing out.

Noah stopped for just a moment on the porch, taking it all in, his birth mother and her family, his adoptive father and his new wife, his sisters who had welcomed him without hesitation, and Hannah, the woman he loved more than life itself.

He thought about Greg Baker, the father he'd never met, and wished he could have known him. But he also felt grateful for Charles Baker, who had raised him and loved him and shaped him into the man he'd become.

He had two mothers now, one who had given him life and grieved his absence, and one who had raised him despite her own struggles and demons. He had two fathers, one who had died too young with dreams unfulfilled, and one who had been there for every important moment of his life.

He had more family than he'd ever imagined possible. And he was about to start his own family with Hannah.

Noah had spent so many years afraid, afraid of commitment, afraid of repeating his parents' mistakes, afraid of being hurt, afraid of loving too much. But standing here on Christmas Day, surrounded by family and love and the promise of new beginnings, he realized that fear had nearly cost him everything that mattered.

Love was worth the risk. Love was worth fighting for. Love was worth being brave.

And Noah was done being afraid.

"Come on," Hannah said, tugging his hand. "We have twin babies to meet properly at the hospital. Our first official act as aunt and uncle."

Noah laughed, pulling her close for one more kiss before they headed to the car. "I can't wait to meet them. And I can't wait to start our life together, Hannah. Really start it, marriage, babies, growing old together, all of it."

"Me too," Hannah said, resting her head against his shoulder as they walked through the snow. "Me too."

Behind them, Beth called out, "Are you two coming or what? Those grandbabies won't stay little forever!"

Everyone laughed, and Noah felt a happiness so complete it was almost overwhelming.

This was home. This was family. This was love.

And it was the best Christmas gift he could have ever received.

* * *

MERRY CHRISTMAS TO all who celebrate, and to everyone reading this, may your days be filled with love, laughter, and the kind of family that makes every season bright. Thank you for joining Noah and Hannah on their journey home. May we all find the courage to face our fears and fight for the love we deserve.

THE RELUCTANT SANTA

"His soul is mine," Devon, the devil's angel, said. He watched the humans, who were oblivious to his presence, gathered in the sales office. One of the best things about being an angel was his ability to pop into just about anywhere and spy on his subjects without their knowledge. He could observe the humans as if were watching a play and even occasionally act as director.

A chill wind howled outside the downtown Denver office, heralding the arrival of winter and the holiday season. The perfect time of year to increase his soul count. Devon studied his next soul, a brown-haired young man with expressive brows and a quirky grin. Unbeknownst to him, the salesman's life meter was about to expire unless he made drastic changes.

"Devon," a voice echoed into the atmosphere before the being that irritated him the most shimmered into his vision. "Doing a soul count before he's yours?"

Slowly, an angel materialized, clad from head to toe in a white leather jacket and white knee-high boots fit snug over white leather pants. A gold belt around her waist, held a cross that signified sergeant, angel, first class. Her halo was tilted at a rakish angle. In earth terms, Gabriella looked hot.

"Whoever is in charge of your wardrobe, I like the changes they've made," Devon said, letting his eyes rake her until a searing heat reminded him he was crossing boundaries. "Please tell me they ditched the boring robes."

With a toss of her blonde hair, her blue eyes flashed, glinting silver as her brows rose.

"My robes are hardly boring, but no, one of my cases is a motorcyclist. I'm riding shotgun today, trying to keep him from splattering all over the highway. The robes kept blowing up in my face, so I found a solution."

"Nice!" Devon shook his head and forced his eyes back to the human whose life he'd soon influence. "I thought your promotion at Easter took you out of the saving souls division."

Gabriella smiled as the air around her shimmered. Why didn't the angels from purgatory patrol get that shimmery essence?

"Devon, we work so…well together" she said, drawing out the word until he wanted to snap at her. He held onto his temper.

"We're all looking for ways to make quota this time of year. Only the strongest stay out of the pit, and every time I come up against you, I lose. But not this time. This one belongs to me," he announced, staring at the man whose only interest in life was making money. No family, no girlfriends, no friends— just work and money.

Gabriella tsked. "Now why would you want to send this poor man to hell for eternity? He just needs a little coaxing to choose the right path."

Devon sighed. "His time is about to expire. I'm here to collect his soul."

"Maybe," she said. "Unless, I can give him some guidance and save him from evil."

"Not this time. Heavenly angels may not be able to play dirty, but I can," he said, smiling at Gabriella. "And I intend to win this one."

Gabriella laughed.

"Always so arrogant, Devon." She glanced at their human. "His case is challenging, but I'm certain I can help him."

She turned toward Devon, her brows rising. "Playing dirty landed you where you are now. Why should I expect anything less?"

"How I got here doesn't matter. I need this soul," he snapped. "You make your soul count or the big man sends you back to the pit to fight and claw your way back for another chance."

"And Colin McDermott needs to be saved," Gabriella said, swirling back to their subject. "I mean, look at the poor man. He has no idea his priorities are in the wrong place. He's a selfish, greedy man because he's unloved."

"Love!" Devon exclaimed. "You heavenly angels think loving someone solves everything."

Gabriella shook her head at Devon, her blue eyes darkening with some sort of power. "Even you deserved love, Devon. In fact, if I had been your angel, I would found someone to show you love. Hopefully, you'd have been smart enough to grab the lifeline."

"Well, you weren't my angel, and now I'm the big man's soul catcher."

"It's simple, Devon. Why would you want to lure more men into the darkness you already face?" she asked.

Devon clenched his fist, struggling to control the frustration that spiraled through him. Hell was not a place anyone planned on going. "The pit!" he said. "Let's just concentrate on the human."

"I already was." She contemplated Colin McDermott. "He's quite handsome with those long, sandy lashes and sparkling honey eyes. If I were human, one look and he'd melt my heart."

"Women on earth know he's not a good risk. I could wrap this case up before Christmas, if you weren't here."

"Too bad. I'm here to keep you from destroying him," she said, giving him a stern frown. "The poor soul has no idea of what he's about to face. I'm sure you've got some nasty surprises in store for him, some hard to resist temptations. But hopefully, with my guidance, he'll make the changes his life needs."

Devon shook his head. "No, by Christmas he'll be mine. Count on it."

The Reluctant Santa

A Dear John letter, Amnesia and a Second Chance at Love

When a roadside bomb in Kabul, Afghanistan exploded his Humvee, and wiped his memory of the last ten months, Tyler Ferguson is sent home for Christmas. He can't wait to see his fiancée.

When Kelsey opens her door and the man she'd sent a Dear John letter too is standing on her porch, she fears the worst. Until she realizes he doesn't remember the breakup. Has life given her a second chance with the man she still loves? At least until his memory returns.

Available Everywhere!

Jennifer Moss is having a really bad day.... But it's about to get even worse...

Her teenage son's grades have plummeted. Her husband is distant and cold, and now she's received a letter from the child she gave up for adoption twenty-five years ago.

But a knock on the door, spins her world out of control.

Losing everything, she packs up and returns to Mustang Island where the secrets from her past slowly unravel.

And the boy she left behind so many years ago helps her see that this new beginning could be the best thing that's ever happened to her.

But will their secret child unravel their relationship before it has a chance to begin again?

Available Everywhere

Contemporary Romance
Burnett Brides Contemporary Times
Travis
Tanner
Tucker
Joshua
Jacob
Justin
Cameron
Caleb
Cody
Desiree
Burnett Brides Contemporary Box Set Books 5-7
Burnett Brides Contemporary Box Set 8-10
Burnett Brides Contemporary Box Set 11-14

Return to Cupid, Texas
Cupid Stupid
Cupid Scores
Cupid's Dance
Cupid Help Me!
Cupid Cures
**Cupid's Heart
Cupid Santa
**Cupid Second Chance
Cupid Charmer
Cupid Crazy
Cupid's Bachelorette
Cupid Games
Return to Cupid Box Set Books 1-3
Cupid Help Me Box Set Books 4-6
Return to Cupid Box Set Books 7-9
Return to Cupid Box Set Books 10-12

**The Unlucky Bride

Contemporary Romance
My Sister's Boyfriend
The Wanted Bride
The Reluctant Santa
The Relationship Coach
Secrets, Lies, & Online Dating

Bride, Texas Multi-Author Series
**The Unlucky Bride

Coming Home for Christmas
I'll Be Home for Christmas
White Christmas
Santa's Baby
All I Want For Christmas
Box Set

Inheriting An Irish Groom
Inheriting a Scottish Castle

Kissing Oaks Billionaire Brothers
The Cowboy Billionaire's Lucky Break
The Cowboy Billionaire's Fate
The Cowboy Billionaire's Playbook
The Cowboy Billionaire's Secret
The Cowboy Billionaire's Deception
The Cowboy Billionaire's Match
Kissing Oaks Billionaire Brothers Box Set 1-3
Kissing Oaks Billionaire Brothers Box Set 4-6

Lipstick and Lead 2.0
Nailing the Hit Man

Nailing the Billionaire
Nailing the Single Dad
Box Set

Secrets of Mustang Island
Secrets of a Summer Place
Secrets of a Runaway Bride
Secrets From the Past
Secrets of a Reckless Life
Secrets of a Hidden Life
Secrets of a Midnight Letter

Secrets of Mustang Island Novellas
The Summer I Loved You
When We Meet Again
Christmas at Mustang Island

The Langley Legacy
Collin's Challenge

Short Sexy Reads
Racy Reunions Series
Paying For the Past
My Christmas Soldier
Cupid's Revenge

Western Historicals
A Hero's Heart
Second Chance Cowboy
Ethan

American Brides
**Katie: Bride of Virginia

Angel Creek Christmas Brides
**Charity
**Ginger
**Minne
**Cora
Angel Creek Christmas Box Set

Bad Girls of the West
Scandalous Sadie
Ravenous Rose
Tempting Tessa
Nellie's Redemption
Bad Girls Box Set

The Burnett Brides Series
The Rancher Takes A Bride
The Outlaw Takes A Bride
The Marshal Takes A Bride
The Christmas Bride
Boxed Set

Lipstick and Lead Series
Desperate
Deadly
Dangerous
Daring
Determined
Deceived
Defiant
Devious
Lipstick and Lead Box Set Books 1-4
Lipstick and Lead Box Set Books 5-9
Lipstick and Lead Box Set Books 1-9
**Quinlan's Quest

Mail Order Bride Tales
**A Brother's Betrayal
**Pearl
**Ace's Bride

Scandalous Suffragettes of the West
**Abigail
Bella
Mistletoe Scandal

Southern Historical Romance
A Scarlet Bride

The Cuvier Women
Wronged
Betrayed
Beguiled
Boxed Set

The Debutante's of Durango
The Debutante's Scandal
The Debutante's Gamble
The Debutante's Revenge
The Debutante's Santa
Box Set

**** Denotes a sweet book.**

Want to learn about my new releases before anyone else? Sign up for my New Book Alert and receive a complimentary book.

Sylvia McDaniel is a USA Today Bestselling author with over one hundred western historical and contemporary romance novels under her belt. Known for creating memorable bad boys and good girls who can't help getting into trouble, she spends her days weaving compelling tales filled with heart, humor, and unexpected plot twists. Her family-oriented stories have earned her a loyal fanbase, and she's always dreaming up new ways to keep her readers hooked.

Married to her best friend for over thirty years, Sylvia recently relocated to Colorado, where she enjoys hiking and taking in the natural beauty of the forest that borders their home. Their spoiled dachshund, Zeus (who has his own column in her newsletter), and brat dog Bailey keeps them company on their adventures.

Though their grown son still resides in Texas, Sylvia keeps close ties to her southern roots, especially when it comes to football. A dedicated fan of both the Denver Broncos and the Dallas Cowboys, she's happiest when they're winning.

Love books? Love deals? Love a little mischief? Sign up for my
Substack—it's free!
https://sylviamcdanielauthor.substack.com/
The End